With Glory and Honor

By

Barbara Longstreth Mulkey

AmErica House
Baltimore

[Handwritten inscription across page:] Dec. 2006 To Brenda Colbert With all good wishes, Barbara Longstreth Mulkey

[Handwritten:] MERRY CHRISTMAS DL

[Handwritten:] SPARE ARMY

First printing

ISBN: 1-59129-144-5
PUBLISHED BY AMERICA HOUSE BOOK PUBLISHERS
www.publishamerica.com
Baltimore

Printed in the United States of America

For
Louis

TABLE OF CONTENTS

A FUTURE AND A HOPE

January

JANUARY 1

Scripture Reading: Jeremiah 29:11-13

Verse for the Day: "For surely I know the plans I have for you, says the Lord, plans for your welfare and not for harm, to give you a future with hope." (Jeremiah 29:11)

A Future and a Hope

The football team is on a roll;
they've lost ten in a row.
But they approach each Saturday
with fervent hope in tow.

The patient gardener tends the soil;
she's bound by gardener's oath
to do her part, then, live with hope
that God will give the growth.

The little boy who's just found out
that Santa is not true
is hopeful still that next Yuletide
he shows up right on cue.

The hope we live with keeps us free
from wasting time in fear.
We face the future willingly
and welcome each new year.

Thought for the Day: The Lord has plans for me, plans for good and not evil. With this knowledge I will approach the future with hope.

JANUARY 2

Scripture Reading: Matthew 6:25-34

Verse for the Day: "So do not worry about tomorrow, for tomorrow will bring worries of its own. Today's trouble is enough for today." (Matthew 6:34)

One Day

If, just for today, I can believe
the blue sky overhead is for me;
if I can shed my pessimism,
my doubt, and my anxiety

If, just for today, I can forget
the nagging worries that pursue
and concentrate on acts of kindness
and helpful deeds I need to do

If, just for today, I can persist
in counting the blessings that are mine ...
can keep my spirit tuned to joy
and lose myself in love divine

If, just for today, I can manage
to focus on *now* as the way
I may, at last, have learned to live
one day at a time every day.

Thought for the Day: "One day at a time," will be my prayer, and in this one day, I will endeavor to live so that I will have no regrets when it becomes yesterday.

JANUARY 3

Scripture Reading: 2 Corinthians 1:1-7

Verse for the Day: "Blessed be the God and Father of our our Lord Jesus Christ, the Father of mercies and the God of all consolation, who consoles us in all our affliction, so that we may be able to console those who are in any affliction with the consolation with which we ourselves are consoled by God." (2 Corinthians 1:3-4)

Understanding

I may not live with crippling pain or limb
that does not work or eyes that cannot see;
I may not face the future with a grim
and hopeless longing for what cannot be

but I can be perceptive and alert
to those whose lives are spent along the fringe
of sociability ... those who hurt
those from whom the insensitive might cringe.

I cannot grant fulfillment of desire
for wholeness or release from hopelessness;
I cannot banish fear that something dire
of consequence might add distress.

But this I know—for as long as I live
the gift of understanding I can give.

Thought for the Day: I will be more sensitive to those around me. Today I will reach out and touch someone in need of understanding.

JANUARY 4

Scripture Reading: 1 John 3:1 I-17

Verse for the Day: "Whoever does not love abides in death." (1 John 3:14b)

To Love

Who sees an eagle soar
and smiles at envied flight,
feels heartstrings plucked by freedom's call,
loves life beyond mere sight ...

Who walks the shaded paths
beneath the mighty oaks,
feels pull of nature's eminence,
loves peace the earth invokes ...

Whoever loves lives well
with sight beyond and peace
which passes all understanding
and grows with love's increase.

Thought for the Day: My goal today is love, with compassion and kindness expressed in desire and deeds, toward the best for everyone.

JANUARY 5

Scripture Reading: II Chronicles 15: 1-12

Verse for the Day: "The Lord is with you, while you are with him. If you seek him, he will be found by you ..." (II Chronicles 15:2)

Seek First

The morning papers tell of burglary,
mugging, murder, arson, and extortion,
embezzlement, abuse, and savagery,
in detail out of all proportion.

Remaining optimistic and enthused
takes an extraordinary effort
while being consistently over-newsed
with tabloid tales and lurid, stark report.

The headlines lead us to conclude that hope
is in a bucket headed straight for hell.
Yet, we believe God's hand still holds the rope;
if we hang on in faith ... all will be well.

The answer lies not in the daily news,
but in the daily company we choose.

Thought for the Day: Today I will seek God first and pray that those whose lives are torn by violence will abide in the hope and deliverance that faith offers.

JANUARY 6

Scripture Reading: Acts 12:25; 13:13; 15:36-41

Verse for the Day: "... Barnabas took Mark with him and sailed away to Cyprus. But Paul chose Silas and set out, the believers commending him to the grace of the Lord." (Acts 15:39b-40)

Failure

> When Mark failed Paul, who trusted him,
> and left the mission,
> the chief apostle banished him
> with deep suspicion ...
> and left to Barnabas the task
> of restoration.
> Then Mark, redeemed, wrote the Gospel's
> first presentation.
>
> I have often failed ... let someone
> and myself down ... then,
> felt abandoned, without hope, yet
> moved to try again
> by notable failures like Mark.
> If failure is meant
> to motivate achievement, could
> be it's heaven sent!

Thought for the Day: I will not be side-tracked by failure. However difficult, I will pick myself up, take heart from the example of Mark, and try again.

JANUARY 7

Scripture Reading: II Corinthians 12:7b-10

Verse for the Day: "My grace is sufficient for you, for power is made perfect in weakness." (II Corinthians 12:9)

The Answer

When the Lord says, "No" or "Someday,"
and I say, "Yes" and "Now" ...
when the answer comes, "Trust and obey,"
and I reply, "No how!"

When my prayers seem inefficient,
or I can't get started ...
when God's help seems insufficient,
and my plans are thwarted ...

When I suffer from impatience,
mouthing child-like complaints,
and my whining self-indulgence
would unsanctify saints,

there appears just one solution
to my predicament:
sincerely pray, "Thy will be done,"
as did the One God sent.

For Christ, when needing strength, would kneel
and pray, "Not mine, but thine."
Then through God's grace the Son would feel
the power of the Divine.

Thought for the Day: Today I will not rebel but will accept God's answer after praying sincerely, "Thy will be done."

JANUARY 8

Scripture Reading: I Thessalonians 5:12-22

Verse for the Day: "See that none of you repays evil for evil, but always seek to do good to one another and to all." (I Thessalonians 5:15)

Tempted

When evil tempts by striking first,
I find it hard to resist.
I'm good at getting even
by some diabolical twist.

Once I begin to seek revenge
an inner force compels me
to act in concert boldly
with the evil that repels me.

It's like some hand beyond my own
has scattered my good senses—
has made of right a mockery
and ignored the consequences.

But if I manage to invite
a divine intervention,
then God steps in to shatter all
my evil-inspired intention.

Thought for the Day: Today I will invite God into my life to intervene in any temptation I might face to return evil for evil.

JANUARY 9

Scripture Reading: Psalm 139:1-12

Verse for the Day: "Where can I go from your spirit? Or where can I flee from your presence?" (Psalm 139:7)

No Hiding Place

I am indebted forever to the grace of God.
Every day I realize I'm constrained to be
a prisoner of divine providence and keeping.
Were it not for the Almighty's power to see
some good in this most selfish being, I would surely
need a refuge in which to hide or some way to flee.

A wanderer by nature, I must pray the Lord
to bind my spirit to the Holy; to keep
it fettered, lest I leave the courts of heaven
and, in mortal rebellion, reject God's love and leap
blindly into the abyss where hate and fear preside,
nourished by guilt ... for what we sow, we ought to reap.

I would pray the Lord my soul to take; my heart
to seal that it might be kept in worthiness;
though I know there is none worthy of God's grace,
yet none able to escape mercy offered in excess
by a Sovereign who is far more willing to give
than we are to ask ... whose love is limitless?

Thought for the Day: I will accept the fact that there is no hiding place from the Lord who knows everything about me and still offers unconditional love. I will rejoice in God's grace.

JANUARY 10

Scripture Reading: Psalm 1

Verse for the Day: "... their delight is in the law of the Lord, and on his law they meditate day and night." (Psalm 1:2)

Meditation

The flowing stream of meditation
from ideas in a good book
provides renewal all mystics know ...
swimming often in the brook.

The psalmist, too, provides a witness.
Meditating on the word
makes him like a tree firmly planted
by waters with roots interred
where endless supply of sustenance
is provided.

It does take
a quiet time alone with pages
of affirmation to make
a residual resource which moves
from root, through trunk, to branches,
and out to leafage of lovely life
in fruitful avalanches.

Thought for the Day: Thomas a Kempis said, "I have no rest but in a nook with the Book." There are many good books, as well as the Book, on which to feed. I will feast today!

JANUARY 11

Scripture Reading: Psalm 39

Verse for the Day: "I said, 'I will guard my ways, that I may not sin with my tongue.'" (Psalm 39:1a)

To Complain or to Confess?
That is the Question!

We can't confess while we complain,
and yet, confession's what we need.
Complaints are parasites which feed
upon the soul with brash disdain.

Confession is restorative;
it's good for body and for soul.
Confession humbles; makes the whole
of life inspired, affirmative.

Complaints imply it's all "their" fault ...
the someone else we choose to blame.
Complaining serves but to inflame,
and nagging bitterness exalt.

We can't complain while we confess ...
it's just as simple as may sound.
The key is also simply found:
confessing more—complaining less.

Thought for the Day: I can't confess and complain at the same time, and I will be more closely linked to God through confession than through complaining.

JANUARY 12

Scripture Reading: James 2:1-10

Verse for the Day: "My brethren, show no partiality as you hold the faith of our Lord Jesus Christ, the Lord of Glory." (James 2:1)

Who's to Blame?

I may not have been unkind,
but the good I might have done
was not done; I could not find
the time.

I did not cause the homeless
to be left out on the streets,
nor did I drive the dispossessed
to crime.

But I should have been concerned
that there were those who needed
so much; I should not have turned
away.

Partiality is sin
where needed help is concerned.
Lord, let the best in me win
today.

Thought for the Day: I will try not to show partiality. Today I will look for opportunities to help the unfortunate.

JANUARY 13

Scripture Reading: Acts 12:1-17

Verse for the Day: "While Peter was kept in prison, the church prayed fervently to God for him ... and when they opened the gate, they saw him and were amazed." (Acts 12:5, 16b)

To Open the Gate

When Peter escaped from prison
his followers were shocked,
for even though they prayed with doubt,
God's purpose was not blocked.

A humorous situation,
but very human, too;
to be amazed when God responds,
and what we ask comes through.

To doubt is not a sinful act;
belief is sometimes hard.
There's no one who has yet achieved
a faith by doubt unscarred.

But praying presupposes that
the Lord responds to prayer ...
so, if we pray most fervently,
an answer will be there.

Thought for the Day: I will pray believing that God's "will" will be done in my life and that doubt will not rule the day.

JANUARY 14

Scripture Reading: Luke 9:51-62

Verse for the Day: "And he sent messengers ahead of him. On their way they entered a village of the Samaritans to make ready for him, but they did not receive him. Then, they went on to another village." (Luke 9:52,56)

Doors

We must not be deterred by one closed door,
or even if another one should slam;
it may be that the Lord has purposed more
for us than learning use of batt'ring-ram.

The game of life is not played on a court
as smooth as concrete leveled perfectly;
it's rather through the halls of some dark fort
where shaky floors and doors creak eerily.

One door may shut as we approach with hope,
but then, another opens without touch;
and who are we to say that we can't cope
with slams we judge too many and too much.

From door to door we must move on aware
that God moves with us through what we must bear.

Thought for the Day: I will accept a closed door as a challenge to find another entrance, but I will keep moving on aware that God's ultimate purpose for me is a full life.

JANUARY 15

Scripture Reading: Matthew 20:29-34

Verse for the Day: "Moved with compassion, Jesus touched their eyes. Immediately they regained their sight and followed him." (Matthew 20:34)

No Self Pity

Love, compassion, pity
are very much a part
of Christ's compelling presence
of God's impassioned heart.

The blind Christ met in passing
asked for his healing touch.
Their anguish moved him deeply;
they needed him so much.

He healed them, and they followed
as Christ continued on
to Jerusalem ... conflict
and a gruelling fate foregone.

The pity he showed others
was never self-directed;
in nothing Jesus ever did
was self-concern reflected.

Thought for the Day: I want to be self-giving and reflect the compassion of Christ in all I do. Today I will avoid any temptation to self-pity.

JANUARY 16

Scripture Reading: I Thessalonians 5

Verse for the Day: "Rejoice always, pray without ceasing, give thanks in all circumstances for this is the will of God in Christ Jesus for you." (I Thessalonians 5:16-18)

Again, I Say Rejoice

When I rejoice and pray,
give thanks and praise
and do not spend my days
in capricious maze ...
things turn out orderly
and well on time.
But discipline for me
is an uphill climb.

Though, when I cease to fret,
and pray instead,
rejoicing as I let
tranquility spread
through my impatient mind,
assurance dawns
that when God's way I find,
doubts will be gone.

I will escape the gloom—
and live in the glow—
if I rejoice in God from whom
all blessings flow.

Thought for the Day: With God's help I will try to rejoice, pray, and give thanks today and every day, believing this is God's will.

JANUARY 17

Scripture Reading: Proverbs 10:1-12

Verse for the Day: "The memory of the righteous is a blessing ..." (Proverbs 10:7a)

Memory

I wish you could have known
my granddad ... seen the way
he greeted friend and stranger
and always tried to say
a kind or encouraging
word to brighten the day.

My memory of him goes
back to when I was small;
when he would let me follow as
he went out to feed all
the livestock or watch as he
milked a cow in the stall.

He made me feel important;
his zest for living spilled
over into songs he'd teach
me. My life is yet filled
with the legacy of rich
harmony he instilled.

Thought for the Day: I will live this day as a blessing to someone else, in memory of those whose lives have been such blessings to me.

JANUARY 18

Scripture Reading: Nehemiah 9:9-17

Verse for the Day: "... you are a God ready to forgive, gracious and merciful, slow to anger, and abounding in steadfast love ..." (Nehemiah 9:17b)

Brooding

Guilt and fear and insecurity
have left a brooding soul in me;
I've tried to work out my salvation
release from self-recrimination.

But always there remains the gnawing
presence of worry, overdrawing
all good intentions. It is crippling;
it sends waves of ill-will rippling.

Must I relinguish my life's control
to feel forgiven, secure, and whole?
Must I give up my long-held grudgements,
my arrogant, ego-ridden judgments?

If God's love is unconditional
but forgiveness provisional
on my forgiving ... I must release
all rancor ... let harmful brooding cease.

Thought for the Day: When I'm brooding, I'm missing God's blessing. Therefore, today, I will not brood but will accept gratefully the love and forgiveness of God.

JANUARY 19

Scripture Reading: Ecclesiastes 3:1-8

Verse for the Day: "For everything there is a season, and a time for every matter under heaven." (Ecclesiastes 3:1)

Pressure

I say I work better under pressure;
from leisure I rebel.
I need excuse for mediocrity
in which I can excell.

The self that likes the pressure is afraid
of quiet times alone;
introspection forces me to confront
the ways I have not grown.

My goals and my performance never meet;
relationships ... a joke;
I've not had time for neighbors or for friends;
I never see kinfolk.

I guess I try to justify myself
by being stressed ... downtrod.
I act as though I'm terribly afraid
I might be fired by God.

Thought for the Day: Today I will strive to unwind; to free my life of unhealthy pressure and stress. I will concentrate on the benefits of taking time for myself and others.

JANUARY 20

Scripture Reading: Psalm 126

Verse for the Day: "Then our mouth was filled with laughter, and our tongue with shouts of joy. The Lord has done great things for us, and we rejoiced." (Psalm 126:2a,3)

Laughter

Laughter is a gift as precious as fine
crystal ... to be handled with greatest care;
not to be wielded to try and outshine
another ... but used as something to share.

So, let my laughter be the kind that lifts
the spirits of all those with whom I laugh;
let them consider it one of the gifts
they treasure most ... given in their behalf.

May I never have to live with regret
that my laugh was aimed as bullet through glass,
shattering fragile ego just to get
attention or praise from the chosen class.

I wish to laugh a lot before I'm through,
but only if you can be laughing, too.

Thought for the Day: May I never laugh at another thoughtlessly or in a condescending way, but be ready to share the joy of laughter whenever it's appropriate.

JANUARY 21

Scripture Reading: Isaiah 65:17-25

Verse for the Day: "Before they call I will answer, while they are still speaking I will hear." (Isaiah 65:24)

The Path of Prayer

Before we call the Lord is ready
with providential will and way,
if we listen for the steady
voice of God through prayer each day.

We call ... not to get God's attention,
but to open lines of praise,
whereby our thoughts can, in ascension,
transcend the dailiness of days.

Desire to pray is put within each,
as Creator has designed,
allowing human beings to reach
the potent power of God's mind.

We grow toward that which we envision ...
as we think, so we become.
To pray or not is our decision:
a path for the adventuresome.

Thought for the Day: Today I will reach for the power of God's mind through the divine channel of prayerful praise. And I will listen.

JANUARY 22

Scripture Reading: Philippians 2:1-13

Verse for the Day: "Let each of you look not to your own interests, but to the interests of others. Let the same mind be in you that was in Christ Jesus..." (Philippians 2:4-5)

Disposition

If my disposition's rotten
and my temper's short,
and I never think of others ...
I'm just not that sort;
if I don't like what I see
when I look real close at me
what, then, can the answer be?

First, I have to want to change me
and decide to start.
Secondly, I have to pick out
some consummate heart ...
model my own after one
who's patient, kind, and fun;
who's goodwill is never outdone.

I must make the Lord a model;
I must have the mind
Christ had. And I need to follow
until being kind
is as natural as air.
Then, before I am aware,
I will come to really care.

Thought for the Day: My disposition is what I will it to be. I will try to imitate the mind of Christ and be pleasant and out-going to all.

JANUARY 23

Scripture Reading: Psalm 138

Verse for the Day: "They shall sing of the ways of the Lord, for great is the glory of the Lord. For though the Lord is high, he regards the lowly." (Psalm 138:5-6)

They Shall Sing

My grandmother used to sing
out in the yard, full throat,
her gospel songs and hymns
to cow and pig and goat.

She would belt out melody
while hoeing black-eyed peas
and green beans in the garden
or pruning red plum trees.

The neighbors always knew when
my grandma worked outside,
though the nearest lived beyond
a meadow half-mile wide.

I'm glad it isn't required
that only well-trained voice
sing hymns of praise on key
in order to rejoice.

Thought for the Day: I will praise God for the memories of voices from the past raised in song and for the hymns that have inspired me.

JANUARY 24

Scripture Reading: Matthew 24:31-51

Verse for the Day: "Heaven and earth will pass away, but my words will not pass away." (Matthew 24:35)

A Word

There's nothing else in all the world
as lovely as a word.
As gorgeous as a sunset is
or radiant redbird,
yet still the word of kindness ranks
as beauty unsurpassed.

For though I marvel at the sight
of snow, it will not last,
and while a tree, in autumn shades
of red and burnished gold
with sunlight playing on the leaves,
is something to behold ...

there is nothing so exquisite
as just the one right word
spoken at the one right moment
it needed to be heard.

Thought for the Day: Words are so powerful, and I know what beautiful words fitly spoken have meant to me. Thank you, Lord, for your words which never fail.

JANUARY 25

Scripture Reading: John 14:1-14

Verse for the Day: "Whatever you ask in my name, I will do it, that the Father may be glorified in the Son." (John 14:13)

To Ask

As any good parent knows
advice is best received
when given after requested ...
till then, it's not believed.

God's "will" awaits our request.
Though laser-aimed our way.
it's beam only reaches us
when we are moved to pray.

Prayer opens wide the channel
makes life and living rhyme.
The message may be "yes" or "no"
or "wait until next time!"

But we will know God's "will"
for our lives and its course
only if we ask for it
directly from the Source.

Thought for the Day: Prayer, at its best, is to ask for God to lead. Today I will not attempt to tell the Lord, but I will ask, then wait in prayer for guidance.

JANUARY 26

Scripture Reading: Job 37:1-14

Verse for the Day: "... stop and consider the wondrous works of God." (Job 37:14)

Wonders

This moming I awoke and found
a sheet of ice on frozen ground.
"No use in trying to get through;
won't be much work done if I do."
So I just put my job on hold
and let myself try to enfold
the beauty of God's wonderland.

Soon daffodils will start to bloom
right there beneath that snow-white tomb.
That frost-draped oak will hold a nest
of redbirds nestled on its chest.
The sleeting winds which hurl ice-breath
portending sign of nature's death
will be dispersed by God's own hand.

This world of marvelous delights
of touch and smell and sound and sight
is such a cache of natural good
it ought to bloom in brotherhood.
And will when earth-folk comprehend
that all are family and friend—
and all together fall or stand.

Thought for the Day: Today I will share my appreciation for the wonders of the earth and try to live in peace with all members of my earth family.

JANUARY 27

Scripture Reading: Psalm 146

Verse for the Day: "I will praise the Lord as long as I live." (Psalm 146:2a)

The Secret

The longer you live
  the longer you can love
  and the longer you love
    the longer you will live.

The more you get
  the more you can give
  and the more you give
    the more you will get.

The more you praise
  the more the power
  the more the power
    the more you will praise.

The secret to living
  is *loving* and *giving*
  and *praising* the Lord
    with *power* the reward.

Thought for the Day: Today I will give praise to God, love more, and give more of myself and my resources, that my life, however long, might be more rewarding.

JANUARY 28

Scripture Reading: John 5:1-13

Verse for the Day: "Do you want to be made well?" (John 5:6b)

Expectation

"Do you want to be made well?"
How often have I prayed
for healing of the spirit,
and yet have always stayed
behind my self-made wall
of insecurity and fear.

I pray for a miracle
believing just in fact.
I ask the Lord for guidance
then continue to act
as though I doubt the promise
that before I call God will hear.

Do I doubt the Lord is willing?
Mistrust the God I ask?
Do I think that the Creator
is not equal to the task?
Do I want to be made well
enough to trust and persevere?

Thought for the Day: Today I will pray with expectation. I will trust that God is able, and I will not be surprised by miracles.

JANUARY 29

Scripture Reading: Psalm 55

Verse for the Day: "Cast your burden on the Lord, and he will sustain you."
(Psalm 55:22a)

Cast Your Burden

When I feel that the weight of the world
is mine to carry alone ...
that the tree of life will never bloom again
that the battle flag has been unfurled,
and with all my hope wind-blown,
I'm consigned to a fight I can't win ...
When I feel that I'm chained to the rack
by troubles unmerited,
and I am beleaguered in body and brain ...

I cast off my burdensome knapsack
of long-harbored fear and dread.
I cast it on God who has promised to sustain.
I let anxiety flow from my mind;
let piety and pride
be expunged by confession of sin and wrong.
I ask the Divine to enter and bind
my will to the Almighty's side.
In release I find restoration and song.

Thought for the Day: I accept God's promise to sustain me. Today I will cast my burdens on the Lord and trust.

JANUARY 30

Scripture Reading: John 15:9-17

Verse for the Day: "... I have called you friends, because I have made known to you everything that I have heard from my Father. You did not choose me, but I chose you." (John 15:15-16b)

Soulmate

Let there be deepening wonder and shared
silences, whereby anxiety is put to rest.
Let there be times when new thoughts are compared;
good books are discussed. Let there be zest
for living marked by personal exchange
of rich experience, beyond the reach
of doubt and envy but within the range
of understanding, empowering each.

Let there be a constant growing toward trust,
with curiosity, laughter, a sigh
of yearning, a journey through tears which must
be part of any friendship, else it die.
This is the way, and there is no other,
to be the true soulmate of another.

Thought for the Day: The friendship Christ offers is that of a soulmate. I will strive to be such a friend today and every day.

JANUARY 31

Scripture Reading: John 6:52-71

Verse for the Day: "So Jesus asked the twelve, 'Do you also wish to go away?' Simon Peter answered him, 'Lord, to whom can we go?'" (John 6:67-68)

But God...

I run and hide,
     but God still finds me;
I'm stressed and tried,
     but God unwinds me.

I've aches and pains,
     but God is near me;
more loss than gains,
     but God will cheer me.

I'm mad and cross,
     but God refrains me;
I twist and toss,
     but God sustains me.

I push and shove,
     but God appoints me;
I spurn God's love,
     but God anoints me.

I am to blame
     if God forgets me;
I've guilt and shame,
     but God acquits me.

Thought for the Day: Today I'll recall God's goodness and mercy to me, and I will remember that no where else is such love to be found.

LIKE A DOVE

February

FEBRUARY 1

Scripture Reading: Matthew 3:11-17

Verse for the Day: "... suddenly the heavens were opened to him, and he saw the Spirit of God descending like a dove and alighting on him." (Matthew 3:16)

The Spark

If you have ever felt the hand of God
when circumstances have ridden roughshod
over you ... or stood in awe before new
birth ... watched sunrise over canyon view
and held your breath at such a splendid scene
or feasted from a symphonic tureen;

If ever you have sensed divine presage
immersed yourself in brilliance from the stage
or held the hand of one you loved at death
and knew that peace was just beyond last breath;
if your heart ever melted at the sight
of tiny birds pushed out into first flight;

If you were ever moved to spirit's tug
upon your soul, however vain or smug
you may become—whatever affluence
you may attain, will all be a pretence.
There's something that your life will always lack
until you feel the spark that draws you back.

Thought for the Day: I will stay close to God today, and if I should encounter someone who is in need of inspiration—who has lost the spark—I will try to meet that need.

FEBRUARY 2

Scripture Reading: Psalm 104:24-35

Verse for the Day: "O Lord, how manifold are your works! In wisdom you have made them all ..." (Psalm 104:24a)

Beauty Experienced

One time I saw the brightest red redbird
and thought that I should never see its peer;
but I've seen others since, and it's occurred
to me that nature's stock is not austere.

I once walked through a formal garden planned
and tended with the hand of practiced care;
the flowers seemed alive with color, and
I knew there was none other half so fair.

Yet, gardens I have since seen evidence
the loving care of gardener's patient hand,
and many qualify, with opulence,
as loveliest. I've come to understand

that nature is not stingy; earth's great store
of beauty is the path to heaven's door.

Thought for the Day: Today I will look for the beauty that is all around and realize that care of the environment, so that it may survive and prosper, is just good stewardship.

FEBRUARY 3

Scripture Reading: Genesis 21: 1-8

Verse for the Day: "God has made me to laugh, so that all that hear will laugh with me." (Genesis 21:6)

With Laughter

I have been called a comedian's
      best friend.
Like Sarah, I laugh at absurdity,
      but then ...
I also laugh at jokes, sometimes before
      the end.
I have been known to laugh at wild slapstick;
      and when
another might not catch the humor in
      the scene,
I've laughed until I cried, then laughed some more
      to think
about the situation afterwards.

      It's mean
to laugh when others are distressed,
      or wink
and giggle at someone's embarrassment.
      But I
just love to laugh when it's appropriate.
      Laughter
is meant to brighten life like sunshine in
      the sky.
I feel great while laughing and renewed thereafter!

Thought for the Day: I know that laughter is good medicine; today I will not be stingy with my supply of cheer and good humor. But I'll always laugh "with" and not "at" another.

FEBRUARY 4

Scripture Reading: Proverbs 22:1-12

Verse for the Day: "A good name is to be chosen rather than great riches, and favor is better than silver or gold." (Proverbs 22:1)

His Kind

No one spoke ill of him
his reputation spotless.
If he had ever harmed
another or caused distress
his conscience would have stung
him like swarming bumblebees.
He was so sensitive
to all nature ... bugs to trees ...
that even when bitten
by rattler, he did not try
to kill, but made excuse that
snakes have every right to lie
on rocks to sun themselves;
it was he who should have been
more careful. Even kids
knew he was special, and when
they could tag along or
spend time in his company,
it was a treat. He loved
home, the land, and family.
There was not room for all
who came to bid him goodbye,
to share their loss, knowing
his kind is in short supply.

Thought for the Day: Today I'll try to identify and appreciate unique qualities of people and creatures.

FEBRUARY 5

Scripture Reading: Deuteronomy 16:15-21

Verse for the Day: "Justice, and, only justice, you shall pursue ..." (Deuteronomy 16:20a)

It Hurts

She smiled weakly when she saw me,
which was not her usual style.
From her wheelchair by the window,
I have seen from a quarter mile
her arm waving like flag flying
when I'd come to visit a while.

But her tears were barely hidden
as I took a seat close by her.
I could feel her fingers tremble;
I knew her heart was in a stir.
The letter handed me was crushed
and nearly tear-stained to a blur.

"Those slant-eyed, yellow gooks will own
America ..." the line began.
They had been pen pals now for months,
but she had not met the woman.
"Would she feel that way if she knew
I'm Japanese-American?"

Thought for the Day: I will do all I can to alleviate the hurt of those who suffer prejudice and to enlighten the prejudiced to the cruelty of such injustice.

FEBRUARY 6

Scripture Reading: John 8:12-20

Verse for the Day: "And again, Jesus spoke to them, saying, 'I am the light of the world. Whoever follows me will never walk in darkness but will have the light of life.'" (John 8:12)

The Light

I've often stumbled in the dark
and cut my knee on rock's sharp edge;
I've scraped my arm on oak's rough bark,
and nearly fallen down the ledge.

I know well what it means to walk
through life in darkness and to flee
from fears too terrible to talk
about, too harrowing to see.

When anguish settles on my life
like storm which falls upon the lake,
and when I feel that winds of strife
will drown me in the billow's wake ...

from God's lighthouse there shines on me
a beam, and if I follow it
in confidence, I'm led to see
a throughway that is brightly lit.

Thought for the Day: I will listen when God speaks to me, and I will always try to follow where divine light leads, knowing it will lead me through the dark.

FEBRUARY 7

Scripture Reading: James 1:1-8

Verse for the Day: "But let patience have its perfect work, that you may be perfect and complete, lacking nothing." (James 1:4)

Prayer for Patience

Dear God:
        Not for me alone
I ask for patience now,
but also for those I'm prone
to yell at and tell how
things always have to be done.

Teach me, Lord, that waiting
is quite often good for one ...
good for cultivating
a feel for introspection
(which is not effortless).

There is so much to be done ...
moments measured in stress.
Help me, God, to center down
gain composure, and then,
erase this constant frown.

Give patience, Lord.
                        Amen.

Thought for the Day: Today I will practice patience and pray for more of the same. Then someday, with God's help, I'll become a patient person.

FEBRUARY 8

Scripture Reading: Matthew 6:9-21

Verse for the Day: "For if you forgive others their trespasses, your heavenly Father will also forgive you; but if you do not forgive others, neither will your Father forgive your trespasses." (Matthew 6:14-15)

To Be Alive

To be alive is to be trusting,
vulnerable to pain and suffering ...
      forgiving to the uttermost ...
forsaking peace to join the cause
of justice at the whipping post ...
      renouncing hunger for applause.

The other option facing mortals
is stepping through extinction's portals.
      Though that way may be paved in gold ...
gold makes a fascinating crypt
for someone caught in scorn's brash fold
      or by contempt of goodness gripped.

To be alive is to be growing,
dependent on the Lord's all-knowing.
      God, help us live while we're alive,
ever trusting, ever trying ...
in forgiving, endure and thrive ...
      and, by your grace, prevail through dying.

Thought for the Day: Today I will be alive to experiences that make living spiritually vibrant ... forgiveness, humility, and the cause of justice.

FEBRUARY 9

Scripture Reading: Matthew 6:1-8

Verse for the Day: "And whenever you pray do not be like the hypocrites; for they love to stand and pray in the synagogues and at the street corners, so that they may be seen by others. Truly, I tell you, they have received their reward." (Matthew 6:5)

God Knows

When we ask the Lord for faith...
we, then, must stand upon it.
It would be insincere if, when
trial or tribulation descend,
we should lose heart and quit.

If faith is real and manifest,
it must survive when needed.
When things are great it's effortless
to preach to others in distress
that our faith has succeeded.

And if we ask for faith then plead,
"Let no troubles come our way,"
it isn't really faith we want,
but ease and plenty from earth's font.
The Lord knows why we pray!

Thought for the Day: I will pray not only for faith, but for the steadfastness to exercise my faith when troubles come.

FEBRUARY 10

Scripture Reading: Isaiah 41-1-10

Verse for the Day: "Do not fear, for I am with you, do not be afraid, for I am your God, I will strengthen you, I will help you, I will uphold you with my victorious right hand." (Isaiah 41:10)

With Certainty

He knew he must let go;
she was so frail
and suffered in the throe
of pain and agony.

He read her silent plea
to end this long travail.

"Do not fear," she had said,
before she had
been mutely trapped in bed;
"God is our help and strength
whatever span or length
of life ... so don't be sad."

He knew that she believed
and was at peace,
though he was sorely grieved.
But, as he felt her slip
from this life's fragile grip,
his fear and doubting ceased.

Thought for the Day: While grief is natural, I will remember that it is not the end. Beyond sorrow is the certainty of God.

FEBRUARY 11

Scripture Reading: Matthew 7:7-14

Verse for the Day: "Enter through the narrow gate; for the gate is wide and the road is easy that leads to destruction, and there are many who take it. For the gate is narrow and the road is hard that leads to life, and there are few who find it." (Matthew 7:13-14)

The Gate

The road was heavily traveled
    by passersby
who never stopped to lend a hand
    or hear a sigh ...
who never realized that they
    were in a rut.
Their self-important carriage was
    a kind of strut.

The back trail was grown over some
    and seemed unused,
and those who chanced it could become
    buffeted, bruised.
But there was laughter on the way
    for those who heard;
and, for one who listened closely,
    sound of songbird.

The road led to a wide front gate
    and tiresome trade.
The back trail's narrow gate led to
    a rich arcade.

Thought for the Day: Today I will choose the road less travelled and take my chances. I will listen for laughter and song and respond to need and to tears.

FEBRUARY 12

Scripture Reading: Romans 5:1-8

Verse for the Day: "... we also glory in tribulation, knowing that tribulation produces perseverance; and perseverance, character, and character, hope." (Romans 5:3,4)

My Choice

Life, in all its vital realities,
produces either bitterness or hope.
Tribulation will leave one soul at ease,
yet another at the end of the rope.

No one dictates my response to trial;
the verdict is never written in stone.
I can face life with courage or denial;
the choice of attitude is mine alone.

I can take lemons and make lemonade,
or I can envy one who got a peach.
I can dream great dreams or try to persuade
myself that all good is beyond my reach.

I can choose to be the lump or leaven.
There's open to each soul both hell and heaven.

Thought for the Day: I realize that what I do with life is more important than what life does to me, so today I will choose perseverance and hope.

FEBRUARY 13

Scripture Reading: Romans 16:16-27

Verse for the Day: "... I want you to be wise in what is good and guileless in what is evil." (Romans 16:19b)

God is Able

Oh, woe is me, I never know
what self of mine is going to show.
Will I be tossed by temperament
or wisely walk through discontent?

Could "guileless" be ascribed to me,
or "cunning" and "duplicity"
be the terms that spell me out ...
let others know what I'm about?

Oh, wretched being that I am,
inclined to self-will and flim-flam;
while right from wrong I know quite well,
white-lies are effortless to tell.

I pray to be of one mind-set
wise in good and guileless yet.
I believe the Lord is able
to remake me ... whole and stable.

Thought for the Day: Today I will try to be of one mind and stay focused on doing good, telling the truth, being genuine, and believing that God is able to use even me.

FEBRUARY 14

Scripture Reading: Galatians 5:1-14

Verse for the Day: "For freedom Christ has set us free." (Galatians 5:1a)

Freedom

"It is bound to happen again, you know,"
I said to one who's been too quick to love.
"You cannot rush relationships and throw
yourself at someone, attempting to shove
a true alliance down a stubborn throat."

But she is sure her way will work out in
the end. She will not hold herself remote
nor be a friend just when she's sure to win.

So today she's crying through another
betrayal. I'll not say, "I told you so!"
She would say I sound just like her mother.

It's true that wisdom comes with age, although,
when we've lost our vulnerability,
we've also lost our freedom to be free.

Thought for the Day: I will try not to be cynical about friendship and will let myself dare to love even though there is always the possibility of betrayal and loss.

FEBRUARY 15

Scripture Reading: III John

Verse for the Day: "Beloved, you do faithfully whatever you do for the friends, even though they are strangers to you." (Ill John:5)

Guest or Host

On greeting someone he would say,
"You're just so glad to see me!"
He meant it to be taken as a joke.
　　　But those who knew him best knew that
　　　he said it quite sincerely
　　　and meant the words exactly as he spoke.

Someone has said that just two kinds
of people fill the whole earth.
By type they are described as "guest" and "host."
　　　Guests feel no urge to comfort, serve,
　　　or love; claim the right from birth
　　　to be served ... their own comfort uppermost.

Hosts, through divine relationship
feel they must serve, not be served.
With God they share responsibility.
　　　Their life's work is to welcome guests ...
　　　offer love that's undeserved ...
　　　and all in genuine humility.

Thought for the Day: Today I will remember that I'm to be a co-host with God to all the guests who come within my circle, making them feel welcome and loved.

FEBRUARY 16

Scripture Reading: Job 15:17-25

Verse for the Day: "I will show you; listen to me; what I have seen I will declare ..." (Job 15:17)

What Is Real

Only what is real to me
can I make real for you ...
only what I hear and see
and know for sure and do.

I watch TV and realize
that there illusion reigns;
I know that it's not always wise
to call such progress gains.

News accounts that fill the air
of violence on the rise
would have us all be so aware
that fear would paralyze.

News of war and crimes of night
are fact, I must admit.
But I just saw a smile so bright,
I bask in the glow of it.

Only what is real to me
can I make real for you.
I must believe hate's gravity ...
but I *know* that smile was true!

Thought for the Day: Today I will share with others what I know to be real: deeds of kindness, words of love, and the radiance of a smile.

FEBRUARY 17

Scripture Reading: Acts 17:16-28

Verse for the Day: "...He, himself, gives to all mortals life and breath and all things. From one ancestor he made all nations to inhabit the whole earth..." (Acts 17:25b, 26a)

The Sun

The sun came up again this morning.
I often wonder why it wants
to rise and see the earth's chaotic
state; hear humanity's cruel taunts.

The mockingbird sings near my window
its cheerful melody belies
the headline in the morning paper
which says an innocent child dies.

Stray bullet—one of too many fired
in urban warfare through the land.
And yet, the crocus bloomed. I marvel
that such signs of grandeur still stand.

When innocence is being slaughtered
by fear and by hate in disguise,
what wonder if the sun, in despair,
some morning should choose not to rise.

Thought for the Day: A better world begins with me, and I resolve that today I will sow seeds of peace wherever I go and with whomever I meet.

FEBRUARY 18

Scripture Reading: Isaiah 40:25-31

Verse for the Day: "He gives power to the faint and strengthens the powerless." (Isaiah 40:29)

When it Happens

When the worst life has to offer
　　　has been met,
the sun does not stop rising ... nor
　　　fail to set.

When the thing we feared most fiercely
　　　comes to be,
still the moon controls the motions
　　　of the sea.

When our world as we have known it
　　　falls apart,
seasons come and go as they have
　　　from the start.

When the heart has borne more trouble
　　　than its share,
it's still beating ... bearing what it
　　　could not bear.

Thought for the Day: I will endeavor to endure hardship, suffering, or loss without being resentful, knowing that the Lord gives strength to bear whatever comes my way.

FEBRUARY 19

Scripture Reading: Deuteronomy 11:8-15

Verse for the Day: "But the land that you are crossing over to occupy is a land of hills and valleys, watered by rain from the sky, a land that the Lord your God looks after. The eyes of the Lord your God are always on it from the beginning of the year to the end of the year." (Deuteronomy 11:11,12)

The Eyes of God

The earth will still turn green when spring has come;
the birds will head for northern fields and feed.
The poet will write lines of verse to some
alliance with the life that's in the seed.

Then temperatures will start their upward climb,
and sudden summer storms will shake the night.
The longer daylight hours will furnish time
to store reflection for the winter plight.

But autumn, first, must make its annual call;
as sure as is the falling of the leaves,
before the winter always comes the fall
and with it wizardry that color weaves.

No matter what the seasons hold in store
the eyes of God will be upon all four.

Thought for the Day: Today I will enjoy the beauty and the natural order of the earth and acknowledge the reliability of God.

FEBRUARY 20

Scripture Reading: 1 Corinthians 4:1-7

Verse for the Day: "What do you have that you did not receive? And if you received it, why do you boast as if it were not a gift?" (1 Corinthians 4:7b)

Who Gets Credit?

He's very intelligent,
everyone says.
He takes all the credit himself.
I've wondered sometimes if he
thinks that his brains
came out of a book on the shelf.

She's pretty and knows how to
manipulate,
preening like a peacock full-fanned.
Has little regard for those
less endowed and
acts as though looks were self-planned.

If talent, ability,
brains, or good looks
are your inheritance from birth,
give the Lord credit; accept
them as gifts, and
make useful your stay here on earth.

Thought for the Day: I will look upon any ability I have and any of the other blessings of life as gifts from God and not of my own doing, and I will use them for good, not just for self-glorification.

FEBRUARY 21

Scripture Reading: Hebrews 2:10-18

Verse for the Day: "Because he himself was tested by what he suffered, he is able to help those who are being tested." (Hebrews 2:18)

Help! Help!

She heard the siren
knew the routine
someone was injured
out on the mean
streets of the city
where rage was law
and where, when questioned
nobody saw
nothin' ... it happened
so fast, and then
one lay there bleeding
to death again.
How do I manage
to raise my son
where teenagers think
right is a gun
and he who has it
should rule the day?
How do I help him
when we must stay
here where our home is?
Lord, it's just you
I must rely on
to see us through.

Thought for the Day: When, through circumstances and situations beyond my control, I am severely tested, I will remember that God is an ever-present help.

FEBRUARY 22

Scripture Reading: Ephesians 4:7-16

Verse for the Day: "He who descended is the same one who ascended far above all the heavens, so that he might fill all things." (Ephesians 4:10)

Fulfillment

A wise man said it long ago
"Christ became what we are that he
might make us what he is." And so,
Christ-like is what we ought to be.

But Christ above all others knew
it would not be an easy thing
to remake human beings who
were willful, mean, and bargaining.

The only way to be Christ-like
is freely choosing self-denial.
And who among us wants to strive
for self-abasement, grief, and trial?

But, recreated in his image
we could not help but share the strife
in the anguished daily scrimmage
of the least who treasure life.

Thought for the Day: I will aim for enough self-esteem to willfully choose self-denial which involves, in Christ-like fashion, loving even the difficult to love and suffering with those who suffer.

FEBRUARY 23

Scripture Reading: Psalm 48:1-14

Verse for the Day: "He will be our guide forever." (Psalm 48:14)

The Guide

He took her by the hand and led her through
the maze of traffic lights past honking car.
"Where do you need to go," he asked, "and who
has left you here alone? Have you come far?"

Mute and deaf she only smiled and gestured.
He understood; her school was near at hand.
He took her there and in that sequestered
sanctuary found the one in command.

The headmaster explained, "She runs away.
She wants to be like other youngsters who
can manage on their own and be okay.
We're lucky you found her or she found you."

The uniformed policeman's smile was wide ...
the best part of his job was playing guide.

Thought for the Day: There are times when I'm called upon to be a guide
for another. Remembering that God is always there as my guide,
I will do my best.

FEBRUARY 24

Scripture Reading: Isaiah 32:1-8

Verse for the Day: "Those who are noble plan noble things, and by noble things they stand." (Isaiah 32:8)

Never Too Late

I plan to start anew today
though I may be the only
one who travels down this way
where unknown lurks and shadows play
and I am scared and lonely.

I plan to stop beside the brook
and let my bare feet dangle
in waters cool where big fish look
at me—suspicious of a hook—
while my nerve-ends untangle.

I plan to empty soul of guilt
by kneeling near the willow
whose weeping leaves contritely wilt
like teardrops from my eyes have spilt
in penitence on my pillow.

I plan to ask the Lord above
from whom my life's been riven
to lift my guilt on white-winged dove,
restore my faith, enliven love,
and judge my past forgiven.

Thought for the Day: I will begin today to think more noble thoughts, to act and react more nobly, and with God's help to plan only noble things.

FEBRUARY 25

Scripture Reading: II Corinthians 7

Verse for the Day: "Nevertheless God, who comforts the downcast, comforted us." (2 Corinthians 7:6)

Moods

Pretence can mask the way we're feeling.
 A smile can hide a broken heart.
We answer "fine" without revealing
 that we're about to fall apart.

But, if observed in private moments,
 the mood we're in is soon revealed;
the frown, the slump, the glum endowment
 of a word that anguish yields.

The eyes reflect emotion's mood swings;
 they sparkle when we're feeling fine.
The shoulders lift; an easy laugh brings
 body and psyche in align.

When the melancholy mood descends
 God can provide wings for the flight
back to morning ... nighttime ends
 when we discover divine light.

Thought for the Day: Today I will try to live in divine light, seeking help for dark moods in the insight provided me and those who would help me.

FEBRUARY 26

Scripture Reading: Philippians 1:21-30

Verse for the Day: "For he has graciously granted you the privilege not only of believing in Christ, but of suffering for him as well—since you are having the same struggle that you saw I had and now hear that I still have." (Philippians 1:29-30)

Conflict

I cannot live in conflict!
To disagree is one thing,
but some stubbornly inflict
enmity and bickering
into the situation.
That's another!
And I know
that, while sanctification
requires suffering to show
faithfulness, I may not get
to be a saint if conflict
has to be the heart of it.
In valor I'm derelict.
The apostles had to face
confrontation everywhere—
insult, scorn, abuse, disgrace—
bearing much more than their share.
They faced martyrdom with pride.
Cowardly, but most precise,
I ask forgiveness for I'd
be for peace at any price.

Thought for the Day: Since conflict is a part of life, I pray I'll be able to handle it without enmity or the shirking of responsibility.

FEBRUARY 27

Scripture Reading: Romans 12:1-5

Verse for the Day: "Do not be conformed to this world, but be transformed by the renewing of your minds, so that you may discern what is the will of God—what is good and acceptable and perfect." (Romans 12:2)

Transformed

We're not to let the world around us
squeeze us into its mold,
but rather, by the mind's renewal
discern the good and hold
the will of God as our intention
until we are made bold.

I think timidity of witness
results from mixed-up mind;
should I reach out and take a chance when
I'm not sure what I'll find,
or play it safe with no risk getting
myself into a bind?

The people I admire supremely
are those whose words are spare,
while their hands and feet keep busy
in an effort to share
themselves. I pray for transformation;
Lord, make me want to dare.

Thought for the Day: Renew a right mind within me, Lord, that this day I will be empowered to do good, be acceptable in your sight, and strive for perfection in spirit.

FEBRUARY 28

Scripture Reading: Genesis 1:1-13

Verse for the Day: "The earth brought forth vegetation: plants yielding seed of every kind, and trees of every kind bearing fruit with the seed in it. And God saw that it was good." (Genesis 1:12)

The Show Goes On

It must have been a lovely day
when God made vegetation ...
at least most colorful, I'd say,
of all days in creation.
The spoken word caused trees to form
with trunks as strong as mountains
and flowers spring from red-earth loam
like water from a fountain.

Great joy must have filled the heart
when fruit was freshly savored ...
the pure delight of apples tart
or purple grapes sweet-flavored.
While resting on the soft green turf,
for sure I am aware
that God impelled the rising surf
and ordered sunshine fair.

But trees and flowers, fruits and grass,
all colors of the rainbow ...
when God spoke these, there came to pass
earth's most spectacular show!

Thought for the Day: I will not take the beauty of the earth for granted; rather, I will treasure each day as a showcase for God's bounty.

FEBRUARY 29

Scripture Reading: Ecclesiastes 12:1-13

Verse for the Day: "The end of the matter; all has been heard. Fear God, and keep his commandments; for that is the whole duty of everyone." (Ecclesiastes 12:13)

The Visit

He visited with her
as friendly as could be.
With animated smile
it hardly seemed that he
was that same fellow who
would, scowling, look through me.
    His manner always put
    me off as I passed by;
    I'd never tried to speak
    or even catch his eye,
    fearful of rebuttal.
    I've always been quite shy.
Then, as she turned to leave,
I heard him say, "Thank you
for talking here with me."
And she said, right on cue,
"My pleasure!" Then, I thought,
it should have been mine, too.
    His frown was just a front;
    his stare, protective guise.
    Who knows what causes masks
    or what pain underlies?
    Next time I'll smile and speak
    to both of our surprise!

Thought for the Day: When all is said and done, it won't matter how others respond to me, but how I respond to others, and in so doing, to God.

WITH GLORY AND HONOR

March

MARCH 1

Scripture Reading: Psalm 8

Verse for the Day: "When I look at your heavens, the work of your fingers, the moon and the stars that you have established; what are human beings that you are mindful of them, mortals that you care for them? Yet you have made them a little lower than God and crowned them with glory and honor." (Psalm 8:3-5)

Why?

I have never known why
cloud figures grace the sky,
or why the mocking bird
repeats each song he's heard.

I have never comprehended
how rainbow hues are blended,
or why a tree grows tall
from a seed so very small.

I'll never figure out
what airwaves are about,
or how wildflowers know
where they're supposed to grow.

But I tend to look askance
at the notion that it's chance
or just artistic blunders
that called forth all these wonders.

Thought for the Day: I will be aware today of the many marvels, including human beings, which are the result of God's creative work.

MARCH 2

Scripture Reading: Deuteronomy 8: 1-10

Verse for the Day: "You shall eat your fill and bless the Lord your God for the good land that he has given you." (Deuteronomy 8:10)

Here and There

When I survey the land on which I live,
the paths I walk along through wooded stretch,
the strawberries (to which I'm sensitive)
that grow in patch designed for artist's sketch ...

I wonder if there is another place
as beautiful and rich in natural
resources and as filled with Godly grace
as is this terra firma miracle.

And yet, I know that other lands are fair
and dear to those whose roots are in the soil
of distant ground, whose constancy is where
they feel the tug of conscience to be loyal.

The Lord invites all people ... come and dine!
Earth's bounty is to bless your land and mine.

Thought for the Day: I will appreciate all the beauty of the land I call mine but not overlook the rights and needs of those equally as loyal to other lands.

MARCH 3

Scripture Reading: I Corinthians 16

Verse for the Day: "Let all you do be done in love." (I Corinthians 16:14)

Saving

He saves old magazines and articles
from newspapers that lay
in stacks beside the bed and under it,
and campaign signs that say,
FRANKLIN D. ROOSEVELT For PRESIDENT;
he's peculiar that way.

He keeps bread wrappers, balls of foil and string,
and even broken tools;
his cabinets are full of jars and lids,
bent nails, and empty spools
that he might need. He smiles when visiting
relative ridicules.

But he is kind and never hesitates
to offer what he's got
that someone else might need, nor fail to help
brighten another's lot
by sharing things. Thank God for thrifty heads
on those who hearts are not!

Thought for the Day: Today I will try not to judge another for what I consider peculiar ways, but rather be thankful that there are always those willing to share.

MARCH 4

Scripture Reading: Luke 19:1-10

Verse for the Day: "For the Son of Man came to seek out and to save the lost." (Luke 19:10)

Intercessory Prayer

For all the homeless people
who walk the streets and wait
for nothing in particular,
I pray it's not too late.

For children who are hungry,
whose plight is often seen
as just inevitable,
let mercy intervene.

For those alone and lonely,
through no fault of their own—
but simply as survivors—
may seeds of care be sown.

For those who are imprisoned,
with lives by misuse marred,
grant reconciliation.
In *their* pain, *all* are scarred.

For friends and loved ones nearby
and those so far away,
my heart beats in a prayerful
intercession today.

Thought for the Day: I will remember that prayers of intercession are an effective means of reminding me of my responsibility to those for whom I pray.

MARCH 5

Scripture Reading: Philippians 3:7-14

Verse for the Day: "... forgetting what lies behind and straining forward to what lies ahead, I press on toward the goal of the heavenly call of God in Christ Jesus." (Philippians 3:13b-14)

Press On

We've all done things we're sorry for,
some things we would undo;
but if we dwell on past mistakes,
we'll rue the present, too.

We must forget what lies behind;
press on to what's ahead.
Our task is living each today;
the past is done and dead.

We profit from mistakes if we
have learned what not to do,
and how to spend our precious time
with goals and motives true.

If God forgives and clears the slate
and calls for us to dwell
in present light ... not prior night ...
why keep ourselves in hell?

Thought for the Day: I will try to forget my past mistakes and misdeeds, accept God's forgiveness, and forgive myself. I will move on into the light.

MARCH 6

Scripture Reading: II Timothy 2:16-23 .

Verse for the Day: "Have nothing to do with stupid and senseless controversies; you know that they breed quarrels." (II Timothy 2:23)

Takes Two to Quarrel

Lord, let me not be so inclined
    to take offense,
to judge another's attitude
    as evidence
that offered friendship is a farce,
    a mere pretense.

It may be that he's had a day
    so hard that he's
short-tempered, tired, indifferent,
    and hard to please.
But I, also, have had some days
    like one of these.

Let me, instead of lashing out
    and fighting back,
put myself in his place, acquire
    the subtle knack
of easing tension by taking
    a gentle tack.

Thought for the Day: Today I will not strike back or respond harshly when tempted to, but rather, I will strive to be a peace-maker.

MARCH 7

Scripture Reading: Ephesians 3:14-21

Verse for the Day: "... that you may be strengthened in your inner being with power through his Spirit, and that Christ may dwell in your hearts through faith, as you are being rooted and grounded in love." (Ephesians 3:16b-17)

No Argument

Sometimes I sound so adamant
that I would scare away
those who might challenge with dissent
or have another say.

If I've offended, I lament
that my convictions hold
so fast my energies are spent
preserving my own mold.

For truth is multifarious,
depending on the place
from which one starts the various
pursuit of saving grace.

But God's *truth* will at last win out,
however tried and tossed.
It will prevail, without a doubt,
and not one grain be lost.

Thought for the Day: I will try to be tolerant of other people's views, while hanging on to my own convictions, and trust God for the ultimate truth.

MARCH 8

Scripture Reading: Psalm 37:1-11

Verse for the Day: "Be still before the Lord, and wait patiently for him ... Do not fret—it leads only to evil." (Psalm 37: 7a,8b)

Fretting

I am a worrier,
I confess;
as such I'm constantly
in restless
temper, nerves frayed and mood
unduly
swayed by fears and judgments
unruly.

My imagination
running wild
disguises the truth that
I'm God's child.
Lord, help me trust you and
not to fret;
But then, worry me if
I forget.

Thought for the Day: I know quality living is not possible if fretting has become a way of life. I must replace worry with such trust in God that there is the stillness of peace within my being.

MARCH 9

Scripture Reading: Psalm 72

Verse for the Day: "May the mountains yield prosperity for the people, and the hills, in righteousness." (Psalm 72:3)

The Mountains

He loved the mountains
where bobcat and black bear
haunted crevices and dens
where famous outlaw pair
by legend hid their loot.

But it was not for treasure,
for trophy, or game to shoot
that brought him back ... but knowledge
of strength the mountains held
and rightness with the world ...
a joy unparalleled.
He felt his spirits hurled
heavenward ... his fears quelled.

It was in the mountains
that he was moved to pray,
and there God's flowing fountains
spilled righteousness his way.

Thought for the Day: I will lift up my eyes and my heart today, that I might reach the mountaintop; and, when possible, I will spend time in the hills.

MARCH 10

Scripture Lesson: James 3: 1-12

Verse for the Day: "From the same mouth comes blessing and cursing. My brothers and sisters, this ought not to be so." (James 3:10)

Words

Regard the words you use with tender care;
you'll find that they return to taunt or bless.
With force of blow or touch of mild caress,
you'll meet those words you've uttered everywhere.

The things I've later wished I had not said
have filled my nights with tossing, turning, tears,
and troubled thoughts that magnified my fears
and left me facing daylight with sheer dread.

But words I've spoken in a wiser vein
have let me sleep unhindered by remorse
and proved to be a comfort and a source
of strength and peace of mind I would attain.

When words are needed nothing else will do;
but just remember they come back to you.

Thought for the Day: Today I will endeavor to hold in check my hasty judgments and quick temper. I will speak kindly to and about everyone.

MARCH 11

Scripture Reading: 1 Corinthians 13: l-7

Verse for the Day: "If I speak in the tongues of mortals and of angels, but do not have love, I am a noisy gong or clanging cymbal. And if I have prophetic powers, and understand all mysteries and all knowledge, and if I have all faith, so as to remove mountains, but do not have love, I am nothing." (1 Corinthians 13: l-2)

Resolution

The diplomats throughout the world proclaim
advantages of process over threats,
the "peace process" they call it, and the aim
is solving problems before war besets.

Yet, all the rhetoric does not remove
the anchor weighing people down with fear;
and talk alone will not ensure the smooth
and peaceful sail through tranquil waters clear.

For while the minds of genius conquer stars,
put astronauts in space and on the moon,
they cannot find a surer way than wars
nor make the earth, to violence, immune.

The resolution is not hard to find—
it's God's love in the heart of humankind.

Though for the Day: Today, I will let my mind dwell on the possibilities that are open to me to be a force for peace if I let God's love shine through me.

MARCH 12

Scripture Reading: Titus 3:1-7

Verse for the Day: "Remind them to be subject to rulers and authorities, to be obedient, to be ready for every good work, to speak evil of no one, to avoid quarreling, to be gentle, and to show every courtesy to everyone." (Titus 3:1-2)

Do-Gooders

When the term "do-gooder" is used to mock
someone with whom we strongly disagree,
perhaps we need reminding that the clock
of doing good runs down for you and me.

Was said of Christ he went about the task
of doing good, and who would dare to say
that those who take him seriously mask
a secret plan to have things their own way?

We call them "bleeding hearts" who go about
responding to great need with empathy.
To cover our own lack of care, we tout
personalized responsibility.

When judgment comes I'd like it said my part
was as a "do-gooder" with "bleeding heart."

Thought for the Day: I will strive for a more compassionate spirit, and I will never denigrate another's efforts at doing good.

MARCH 13

Scripture Reading: Matthew 6:19-26

Verse for the Day: "Look at the birds of the air; they neither sow nor reap, and yet your heavenly Father feeds them. Are you not of more value than they?" (Matthew 6:26)

Inspiration

Whenever I see birds in flight
I am amazed at the insight
that comes to me—I can fly
in mind and put to wings my
words in patterned poetry.

For birds, which waft on winds or
glide above the draft, restore
in me the confidence to
rise above the mundane hew
and cry of adversity.

Folks who seldom lift their eyes
to follow birds through the skies
may not know they, too, have wings—
imagination which flings
them toward creativity.

Hear a bird call as it soars
over trees or across shores
and feel the impulse to try,
to break the bounds, to defy
the odds, to take wings ... to be!

Thought for the Day: Today I will take time to watch the birds in flight, to hear their songs, and to absorb inspiration—then act on it!

MARCH 14

Scripture Reading: Romans 3

Verse for the Day: "... all have sinned and fall short of the glory of God." (Romans 3:23b)

Sin

I know what sin is all about:
it's murder, theft, and mayhem;
it's jealousy, unbridled lust,
and attitudes which I condemn.

There's not a doubt in my own mind
that I can spot sin any time ...
tell by sight who's innocent,
and who is guilty of the crime.

The sinner has a look of stealth,
a furtive, mean, deceitful pose.
Us good guys are all nice, clean-cut,
and shun the company of those.

I know that sin is virulent,
most anyone can feel its pall.
But "all have sinned" comes as a shock,
if I'm included in the "all."

Thought for the Day: I acknowledge that sin is willful disobedience to God, and I, along with everyone else, am in need of God's forgiveness.

MARCH 15

Scripture Reading: Proverbs 3:27-25

Verse for the Day: "... he blesses the abode of the righteous." (Proverbs 3:23b)

The Neighbor

Her house is just as tidy
as she herself has always been
and open to the friendships
she cultivates with genuine
concern and discipline.

She knows that housework requires
diligent, daily attention
as does friendship; and she takes
pride in seeing that both are done
with good humor and fun.

To see the starched white curtains
in windows cleaned to fare-thee-well,
and she, herself, dressed to call
on neighbors ... the ritual
inspirational.

I think she is the kind whom
the Lord would recognize as "good,"
a humble, loving servant.
I only wish that I could
be in that neighborhood.

Thought for the Day: This day I will cheerfully tackle those jobs around the house I've put off, and I will not neglect my friends.

MARCH 16

Scripture Reading: Psalm 32:1-11

Verse for the Day: "I will instruct and teach you in the way which you should go; I will counsel you with my eye upon you." (Psalm 32:8)

The Eyes

> I met your eyes and knew
> that you were kind;
> "compassion" was the word
> which came to mind.
>
> A telescope, the eye
> exposes what
> is in the human heart—
> and what is not.
>
> Your eyes reveal that your
> heart's eye has met
> the guiding eye of God
> and holds it yet.
>
> I only pray my eyes
> disclose a heart
> in which God's counsel rules
> its every part.

Thought for the Day: Today I will seek to meet the eye of the Lord through prayer, and I hope to hold God's counsel so securely in my heart that it will be revealed in my eyes.

MARCH 17

Scripture Reading: Proverbs 17:13-17

Verse for the Day: "A friend loves at all times." (Proverbs 17:17a)

A Friend

All of a sudden she just froze up;
no reason forthcoming ... no blow up.
But she bruskly brushed off my phone call;
said she did not want to talk at all.

I racked my brain for cause specific,
could this be some April Fool's Day trick
in middle March? Had I offended
or could it have been something I said?

I thought she was my friend, for, like me
she had a "funny bone" and would see,
in ordinary situation,
occasion for some laughter and fun.

I see another side of her now,
but I've other sides, too, so I vow
to "hang in there," for I think friendship
ought to be a loving, life-long trip.

Thought for the Day: When something hurtful happens and friendship is strained, I will strive for patience and understanding, and I will try to love at all times.

MARCH 18

Scripture Reading: Luke 6:43-49

Verse for the Day: "I will show you what someone is like who comes to me, hears my words, and acts on them. That one is like a man building a house, who dug deeply and laid the foundation on rock ..." (Luke 6:47-48a)

Rock Bottom

There is a time when hitting rock bottom
is not as bad as one might think;
for when we've finally reached rock bottom,
there is no further down to sink.

We say, derisively, he's hit rock bottom
and should not tarry there at all.
But ridicule is risky business;
pride often comes before the fall.

It behooves us not to be disdainful,
not to heap coals of scom, nor mock.
In fact, Christ likened the wise who heard him
to builders of houses on bedrock.

So, one who's finally hit rock bottom
can start to build a life sincere.
And we must be cautious in our judgment;
things may not be as they appear.

Thought for the Day: I'll try not to pass judgment on one who appears to have hit rock bottom; it may be that it's just a starting place.

MARCH 19

Scripture Reading: Psalm 31:14-24

Verse for the Day: "Be strong, and let your heart take courage, all you who wait for the Lord." (Psalm 31:24)

The Walk

Each day I walk the path—
nine times around—two miles.
Each round I say, "just one more,"
and my "child inside" smiles.

I know that I can make
"just one more" fit and fine,
when even stalwart me
might faint at thought of nine.

Four-and-a-half around—
one mile—might be enough,
but I will not admit
that two miles is too tough.

Besides with "just one more,"
most anything can be
accomplished in due time
satisfactorily.

Thought for the Day: I will remember that almost anything can be accomplished if approached with courage and if I take things one-at-a-time with God.

MARCH 20

Scripture Reading: Proverbs 20:1-12

Verse for the Day:"Even children make themselves known by their acts, by whether what they do is pure and right." (Proverbs 20:11)

Children Know

The children ran along the bank
skipping stones across the pond
when Lollypop, the old man's dog,
came by; and though the kids were fond
of her, they began tossing stones
her way. She yelped when the first one
found its mark, and soon the children,
excited by the sport, had done
their best to render the poor old
hound helpless. That's where Ol' Jeb found
Lollypop so near to death that
she would not survive. The hard ground
where he buried her was close to
his shack. The children never spoke
of the incident but never forgot
that once they had, by stroke
of savage will, taken the life
of one of God's creatures. They knew
right from wrong—they comprehended
life and death—even children do.
And today those children, grown, teach
their own that no moment's pleasure
is worth the loss of a guilt-free
conscience, which is life's real treasure.

Thought for the Day: I pray today for the purity of heart and strength of character that leads me to do the right which I know and have known since childhood.

MARCH 21

Scripture Reading: John 12:20-26

Verse for the Day: "Most assuredly, I say to you, unless a grain of wheat falls into the ground and dies, it remains alone; but if it dies, it produces much grain." (John 12:24)

You Bet Your Life

I had read a book to him;
we played with tiny truck.
Then, when I buckled him in
for the ride home, he struck
my cheek with a kiss, and said,
"Are we pals?" Oh, what luck!

His big brown eyes reflected
the stars up in the sky;
"You bet your life!" I answered,
then waved and said good-bye,
thinking that's what children do—
bet life on such as I.

The same trust is required
as adults daily plod
through ups and downs and sometimes
where angels fear to trod.
With child-like faith undaunted
"you bet your life" on God.

Thought for the Day: I'll endeavor to trust the Lord in all circumstances, knowing that, no matter what the surface conditions, the ultimate result rests with God.

MARCH 22

Scripture Reading: Jude 1-25

Verse for the Day: "But you, beloved, build yourselves up on your most holy faith, keep yourselves in the love of God, look forward to the mercy of our Lord Jesus Christ that leads to eternal life." (Jude 20:21)

Mercy

Looking forward to God's mercy
which means eternal living,
I must in every situation
be merciful in giving.

If I would hold God merciful,
I must demonstrate
that mercy is to me a value
held in high estate.

I must show mercy in responding
to each broken heart,
to every one who has met trouble
and needs a brand new start.

My heart should be as merciful
as manna from above
if I expect God's tolerance
in unconditioned love.

Thought for the Day: Today I will rely on the promise of God that the merciful are blessed and will receive mercy ... and I will try to be one of them.

MARCH 23

Scripture Reading: II Timothy 2:1-15

Verse for the Day: "Do your best to present yourself to God as one approved by him, a worker who has no need to be ashamed, rightly explaining the word of truth." (II Timothy 2:15)

Buffer Zone

When my three sons were very small,
I often prayed that they
would never waste life's precious gifts
or let talents slip away.

Everyone has innate gifts of
wit or ability,
not intended to be squandered
in bloodshed or thievery.

When crime becomes the chosen route
perhaps it is because
creative urge has been denied
approval or applause.

Let music, art, or poetry
be encouraged early on,
and it will serve throughout the years
as a buffer zone.

Thought for the Day: I pray for those who are so desperate that crime seems the way to achievement and those who have never been encouraged in anything uplifting.

MARCH 24

Scripture Reading: Ephesians 6:10-18

Verse for the Day: "Pray in the Spirit at all times in every prayer and supplication. To that end keep alert and always persevere in supplication for all the saints." (Ephesians 6:18)

For These I Pray

For that little boy at the braille keyboard;
that teenager flipping burgers for bread;
for the teacher driven out of her "gourd"
by the students who have to be force-fed.

For that precious baby shaken near death;
the mother frustrated beyond control;
for the paramedic's life-giving breath
to the injured man—poor wretched soul.

For that homeless couple who once lived well;
the migrant child who does not go to school;
for the lonely widow rushing pell-mell
into affairs, being played for a fool.

For these and all others needing a prayer
God, make tomorrow easier to bear.

Thought for the Day: Today, realizing that all things are possible with God, I will pray for those who have such needs and such challenges that answer to prayer may seem to them beyond the realm of possibility.

MARCH 25

Scripture Reading: Luke 6:12-19

Verse for the Day: "And all in the crowd were trying to touch him, for power came out from him and healed all of them." (Luke 6:19)

The Works of God

Christ did not say that he made miracles
but rather that he did the works of God.
The people crowded close around to touch
or even follow in the steps he trod.

They did not know they sought a miracle,
but just that he would heal and make them whole.
The works of God, they sensed, were his to do;
And thus, his touch became consuming goal.

What struggles do we make that Christ could ease?
What temptations face that call for power?
What seems impossible to you and me?
What miracle do I desire this hour?

We, like the crowds, make way to Christ to leave
our cumbered spirits at God's fountainhead,
that we, ourselves, might be the miracles ...
empowered, loved, and uninhibited.

Thought for the Day: Today I will undertake to become a miracle by allowing God's power through Christ to work in me.

MARCH 26

Scripture Reading: Luke 9:23-29

Verse for the Day: "For those who want to save their life will lose it, and those who lose their life for my sake will save it." (Luke 9:24)

The Reason

The boy approached the old man's door at noon.
When Mr. Bob responded to the knock,
two others in the shrubs jumped up, and soon
all three were in the house and teamed to block
escape routes which the frightened man might take.
They ransacked shelves until their bag was full,
and then they ordered the old man to make
them lunch while they made jokes and acted cool.

And just before they left, one boy grabbed hold
a stick of wood from fireplace grate and struck
the head of Mr. Bob who fell on cold
linoleum, and it was just by luck
that he survived. But when police were called
he said he did not want to prosecute
for they were only boys who were enthralled
with "things," which they thought were a substitute

for love which evidently was denied
them early on. "I wish," he said, "that I
might have a chance to talk to them, and I'd
explain the reason Jesus died, or try."

Thought for the Day: I'll try to be more forgiving and understanding ... more loving and patient ... realizing the debt of love I owe.

MARCH 27

Scripture Reading: Mark 9:33-42

Verse for the Day: "For truly I tell you, whoever gives you a cup of water to drink because you bear the name of Christ will by no means lose the reward." (Mark 9:41)

More Than Thirst

Why does he come so often,
that youngster she has hired
to mow the grass in summer,
to ask a drink. She's tired
of answering the doorbell,
but mowing is hard work;
it's hot out there, and she's sure
he doesn't mean to shirk.
Perhaps the boy is needing
someone to hear him out;
his folks are always busy
rushing there and about.
He knows she will not scold him;
she's always been so nice.
She gives him Coca Cola
or lemonade with ice.
Or sometimes just cold water,
but always with a smile,
and most the time she sits down
to talk with him awhile.
I think he knows he's stumbled
across a treasured find
someone who's not judgmental;
someone who's really kind.

Thought for the Day: Today I will look beyond the unreasonable demands on my time. I will be patient with any who might call upon me for help.

MARCH 28

Scripture Reading: John 4:27-42

Verse for the Day: "So when the Samaritans came to him, they asked him to stay with them, and he stayed there two days." (John 4:40)

Real Joy

> I'm busy and feel blessed
> and satisfied to stay
> at work lest minutes flee
> and hours slip away.
>
> But then, the lilting song
> of birds out in the trees
> wafts cross my window sill
> on breath of springtime breeze
>
> I know that we, like birds,
> do best what's done to lift
> the sights of busy souls
> or hearts in aimless drift.
>
> The hours of sharing life
> are also worth employ ...
> and minutes spent with friends
> are those that bring real joy.

Thought for the Day: I know that, to find real joy, sharing time and resources with others must be a part of life. With Christ as example, this will be my goal.

MARCH 29

Scripture Reading: Mark 11:1-11

Verse for the Day: "Then he entered Jerusalem and went into the temple; and when he had looked around at everything, as it was already late, he went out to Bethany with the twelve." (Mark 11:11)

Look Around

When he had looked around at everything...
he saw the Roman conquerors, the priests
who profiteered; he felt the bitter sting
of vanquished masses and knew this must cease.

But he was more than conqueror; he came
to lead the way to life through sacrifice.
And no one understood; they placed the blame
on him, demanding the ultimate price.

What does he feel when he has looked around
the cities where we live and work and play,
where mischief, murder, mayhem run aground,
and troops of good stay side-lined in the fray?

Would he be felled with random, drive-by shot?
Or would his death result from passive plot?

Thought for the Day: Today, I will seek ways to make an impact on the conditions of the community in which I live, knowing that even one person can make a difference.

MARCH 30

Scripture Reading: Mark 12:30-44

Verse for the Day: "Then he called his disciples and said to them, 'Truly, I tell you, this poor widow has put in more than all those who are contributing to the treasury. For all of them have contributed out of their abundance, but she out of her poverty has put in everything she had, all she had to live on.'" (Mark 12:43-44)

Apple Blossoms

> She carried apple blossoms
> to those she called her friends—
> > and "friends" to her meant anyone she met.
> It was not unusual
> for her to spend the day
> > in giving ... and a smile was all she'd get.
> But that was all she wanted,
> for just to know the blooms
> > she cut and carried from her backyard trees
> were now a source of comfort
> was all it ever took;
> > she never was the least bit hard to please.
> A simple, kindly woman,
> she had no worldly wealth,
> > nor had she time nor inclination to
> feel sorry for herself
> or bemoan her lowly state.
> > For she had too much sharing yet to do.

Thought for the Day: Today I resolve not to feel sorry for myself but to find ways of helping other people and spreading goodwill.

MARCH 31

Scripture Reading: John 12:44-50

Verse for the Day: "I have come as a light into the world, so that everyone who believes in me should not remain in the darkness." (John 12:46)

Not News

Often I see
the light
but hide my eyes
despite
knowing that God
is light.

Like child who peek-
a-boos,
my ploy must sore
amuse
the Lord. But it's
not news.

Thought for the Day: I know that God knows me better than I know myself. There is no hiding place from the light.

THE TIME OF SINGING

April

APRIL 1

Scripture Reading: Song of Solomon 2:10-14

Verse for the Day: "For now the winter is past, the rain is over and gone. The flowers appear on the earth; the time of singing has come..." (Song of Solomon 2:11-12a)

Praise for April

God blessed the earth with springtime...
gave April to the world:
the winter months of harboring
are over—life's unfurled.

The songs of birds returning
from migrant journey south
are like the psalms of gratitude
which spring from heart to mouth.

For I have weathered winter
and found the strength to bide
my time till dogwoods, white and pink,
fill yards and countryside.

I know there's nothing fairer
than nature green-impearled.
God blessed the earth with springtime...
gave April to the world!

Thought for the Day: Grateful for the renewal of the earth, I will remember to thank God from whom April blessings flow.

APRIL 2

Scripture Reading: I Timothy 6:11-20

Verse for the Day: "As for those who in the present age are rich, command them not to be haughty or to set their hopes on the uncertainty of riches; rather on God who richly provides us with everything for our enjoyment." (1 Timothy 6:17)

"Do Not Pick the Flowers!"

Needing a respite from work, I took a stroll through the garden.
Perfume and color of lilacs filled the air like a blast from bombardon
blaring from bandstand by the river in the park,

Dreaming of places exotic and romantic I began to embark
on a journey rich in color and odor and sensuous music.

Until... "Hey, you, don't you know you can't pick ..."

Dumbfounded, I stammered ... "What did you say?"

"The flowers!" he shouted. And there in my hand was the lilac bouquet.

Thought for the Day: I will remember to enjoy the natural riches of parks and public gardens as a gift, but I'll leave the beauty as found for others to enjoy.

APRIL 3

Scripture Reading: Genesis 1:20-23

Verse for the Day: And God said, "Let the waters bring forth swarms of living creatures, and let the birds fly above the earth across the dome of the sky!" (Genesis 1:20)

Little Bird

Little bird, little bird, who taught you to sing?
Who showed you the way to rely on the wing?
Little bird, little bird, perched on the limb ...
Was it the same One who taught fish how to swim?

Mocking bird, mocking bird, how did you learn
to imitate sounds so the ear can't discern?
And beautiful cardinal in red cloak and crown
who dressed you so royally with name of renown?

Little bird, little bird, I can tell by your nod ...
you think as I do ... it was God!

Thought for the Day: How blessed I am to live in a world of color and singing. I will remember to give credit for the earth's wonders, big and little, to God.

APRIL 4

Scripture Reading: Jeremiah 17:7-14

Verse for the Day: "Heal me, O Lord, and I shall be healed."
(Jeremiah 17:14)

A Prayer for Wholeness

Heal me, O Lord,
from spiteful thought
and hateful attitude;
from jealousy
and ingratitude.

Lead me, O God,
to acts of kindness
and generosity
to views of tolerance
and sensitivity.

Let me be whole...
alive with your spirit,
atuned to your will.
Heal me, O Lord, as
only you can heal.

Thought for the Day: I know that a full and enriched life depends on a relationship with God. I resolve to spend more time in prayer.

APRIL 5

Scripture Reading: Matthew 7:12-20

Verse for the Day: "In everything do to others as you would have them do to you." (Matthew 7:12a)

At Least

Lord, if I've failed
to lend a hand
or been too slow
to understand
or been too quick
to make demand ...
if I've replied
with sharp-edged haste,
judged time spent drying
tears a waste,
or scoffed at someone's
style or taste ...
Lord, let it be
your will that I
at least see one
more sunrise sky
to make amends—
at least to try.

Thought for the Day: Today I will remember the "Golden Rule" and let it be the standard by which I respond to others.

APRIL 6

Scripture Reading: Psalm 4

Verse for the Day: "You have put gladness in my heart ..." (Psalm 4:7a)

Infectious Happiness

> She made me laugh so many times
> I could not say. My paltry rhymes
> could not begin to count the ones
> her humor touched. She favored puns,
> and those about her where she clerked
> just loved to be near as they worked,
> especially when sadness clutched
> their lives, or tragedy touched,
> for she would never let
> her own pain, woe, or worry get
> the best of her or slow her wit.
>
> Heaven now is better for it!

Thought for the Day: There are so many ways to gladden the hearts of those about us. Today I will make a special effort at good humor.

APRIL 7

Scripture Reading: Proverbs 17:17-28

Verse for the Day: "A cheerful heart is good medicine, but a downcast spirit dries up the bones." (Proverbs 17:22)

In a Roadside Restaurant

It was a little country restaurant in Tontitown;
the cashier's laugh caused us to notice her as we sat down.
She joked and called by name most everyone who paid a check,
and her spontaneous good humor caused me to reflect
that there is not enough instinctive mirth in this old world.
Too often all one hears in public place is noise hurled.

Our lunch was just a bowl of brown baked-beans with hot cornbread—
such simple fare, but we were more than full—by laughter fed.
It was by chance we stopped there on that day for nourishment,
but I believe the extra sustenance was heaven-sent.

Thought for the Day: I will remember that laughter is good medicine and much easier to take than pills. Today I will try to project good humor wherever I am.

APRIL 8

Scripture Reading: I Peter 3:8-12

Verse for the Day: "Finally, all of you, have unity of spirit, sympathy, love for one another, a tender heart, and a humble mind." (I Peter 3:8)

Daddy's Grave

We visited my husband's father's grave
and found the weeds were getting out of hand;
we spent the morning trying just to stave
off total overgrowth—donned work gloves and
pulled up those rude trespassers, roots and all.
Then, we decided something should be done
to keep the grave site neat and to forestall
the day when it again was overrun.
So, we began to carry pretty stones—
some rain-washed white—and crystal rocks that could
be used to make, in variegated tones,
a lovely blanket, which we thought looked good.
    My husband's mother called to relay shock:
    "Some darn fool covered Daddy's grave with rock."

Thought for the Day: I will remember that what looks good to me may not look good to another, and I will try to be humbly considerate and tender-hearted toward other views.

APRIL 9

Scripture Reading: Matthew 6:27-34

Verse for the Day: "Consider the lilies of the field, how they grow; they neither toil nor spin, yet I tell you, even Solomon in all his glory was not clothed like one of these." (Matthew 6: 28b-29)

Wild Flowers

I just took a break from my work
to walk on my path through the woods.
I'm not at all sure what it does for my health,
but I know that it does my soul good.
I spotted alongside the path
some flowers as wild as could be;
there were red, purple, yellow, orange, pink, and white,
all face-up and smiling at me.
They welcomed my trek through the trees,
although I trespassed their terrain;
on each round I made, they waved boisterously
and shouted this joyful refrain ...
"Now, don't be a stranger, ya' hear.
Come often, we love company!"
If only they knew how their colorful presence
engendered vitality.
I've nothing but praise for the wild,
the natural, native, untamed.
I wish that I could be as uninhibited,
as guileless and unashamed.

Thought for the Day: I will enjoy the things of nature that uplift and inspire and encourage others to do the same.

APRIL 10

Scripture Reading: I Thessalonians 4:1-12

Verse for the Day: "... aspire to live quietly, to mind your own affairs, and to work with your hands ..." (I Thessalonians 4:11)

In Quietness

There is something sacred in quietness—
a sacrament no sound can explain—
a peaceful collaboration
of heart and brain.

The end result of studied quiet
is creation from imagination's spell—
a song, a sonnet, a picture, a story
to read or tell;

to put together a business venture,
revive an engine that would not start,
design a building, hold a child,
transplant a heart.

That which enhances meaning and beauty
beyond what nature has designed
proceeds from the ritual of contemplation
and quiet combined.

Thought for the Day: Today I will spend a part of my time in quietness, meditating on what is good and creative and helpful.

APRIL 11

Scripture Reading: Ezekiel 33:30-33

Verse for the Day: "... they hear your words, but they will not obey them. For flattery is on their lips, but their heart is set on their gain." (Ezekiel 33:3lb)

In Reality

Do we build our churches high
just to hold those of our kind?
Would the bills often go unpaid
were we class and color blind?

We gather cans of food for those
whose lot in life we would disdain;
but do we really have the time
to share their misery and pain?

Do we often fail to see
one lying wounded on the road,
while looking heavenward
imploring God to lift our load?

Do we flatter and cajole,
talk sympathy in vain,
and while our lips say love,
do we set our hearts on gain?

Thought for the Day: Today I will try to speak and act only from pure motives and thoughts inspired by God's word.

APRIL 12

Scripture Reading: Genesis 8:13-22

Verse for the Day: "As long as the earth endures, seedtime and harvest, cold and heat, summer and winter, day and night, shall not cease." (Genesis 8:22)

The Promise

The seeds planted in springtime
sprout as the Lord gives growth.
In due season harvest follows;
it's all written there as an oath.

Cold winter weather finds fallow
furrows in iced, early dark.
Summer sun following seeding
entices the plant with life-spark.

Daylight for working comes round
following night's web of sleep;
the assurance of ceaseless shift
in orb of time ... the world's keep.

Spring, summer, autumn, winter ...
As long as earth endures.
Day and night are trustworthy ...
these things God's promise secures.

Thought for the Day: I am grateful today for the promise of seasons—and for all of the special enjoyment that each brings.

APRIL 13

Scripture Reading: Psalm 150

Verse for the Day: "Praise him with trumpet sound; praise him with lute and harp ... praise him with strings and pipe! Praise him with clanging cymbals." (Psalm 150:3, 4b, 5a)

Better Than Medicine

Listening to classical music,
can give the morale a classical kick;
can actually prevent one being sick.

Listening to classics one hour a day
could make unnecessary therapeutic outlay;
put psychologists out of business, they say.

And if one tends to lose track or forget,
it's alleged that much Mozart-listening will beget
improvement of memory like a charmed amulet.

No harm in trying; it's certainly cheaper
than counseling and pills or getting in deeper.
Might prompt one to say ... "This idea's a keeper."

Thought for the Day: I know that listening to music which inspires a spirit-uplift could only be helpful, and I will make time to listen.

APRIL 14

Scripture Reading: Romans 8:28-37

Verse for the Day: "We know that all things work together for good for those who love God, who are called according to his purpose." (Romans 8:28)

God Knows Best

It's good that God sometimes says no,
that every wish is not just so;
God's wisdom is our succor, lest
we're ruined at our own request.

It's good that God at times denies
those things for which our fancy cries;
by some desires we'd not be blest,
but ruined at our own request.

It's good that God refuses some
entreaties made to overcome
divine design; we would invest
in ruin at our own request.

It's good that God turns down such pleas
as would defy hallowed decrees
and doesn't leave us, self-possessed,
in ruin at our own request.

Thought for the Day: I will remember that, whatever comes about, it will all work out if God is at the center of the heart.

APRIL 15

Scripture Reading: Psalm 99

Verse for the Day: "Extoll the Lord our God, and worship at his holy mountain; for the Lord our God is holy." (Psalm 99:9)

The Linking

Wild flowers were blooming
green vines were creeping
birds were chirping
willows were weeping
the creek was flowing
squirrels were chattering
buds were bursting
lizards were scattering.

I was walking
in woods for thinking
contemplating
the divine linking
of all things living
God's vast creating.
I paused for praying...
exhilarating!

Thought for the Day: Today I will observe the things of nature that remind me of God's love for the created world and lead to the worship of its creator.

APRIL 16

Scripture Reading: Proverbs 12:17-25

Verse for the Day: "... those who counsel peace have joy." (Proverbs 12:20b)

To Counsel Peace

Peace is not easy,
nor is the desire
to make peace
likely to inspire
admiration
from most friends.
Talking tough
is what sends
adrenalin flowing.
To warn against haste,
counsel peace
is considered a waste
of energy that could
be used for conquest.
Only those who have peace
can stand the test.
But joy is promised
as reward
for those who counsel
accord.

Thought for the Day: I will, with God's help, strive for peace with all others, believing that peace can prevail.

APRIL 17

Scripture Reading: Luke 23:26-46

Verse for the Day: "Then Jesus, crying with a loud voice, said, 'Father, into your hands I commend my spirit.'" (Luke 23-46)

Into God's Hands

She'd lived a long, dry spell
in abject poverty;
but with some charity,
she'd raised her children well.

Late teens, they left the nest,
forsaking neighborhood.
She gave them all she could
and prayed she'd done her best.

"Oh, Lord, into your hand
I put this dear child's fate."
The prayer helped fear abate
as each chose distant land.

With her own spirit, too,
she made the Lord trustee,
as from dark Calvary,
her Savior deemed to do.

Thought for the Day: Today I will put my efforts, my choices, my ambition, my spirit into God's hands and try to abide by the divine will.

APRIL 18

Scripture Reading: Philippians 3:15-21

Verse for the Day: "Only let us hold fast to what we have attained."
(Philippians 3:16)

What's Left?

Can we never go back
to the house on the ridge,
the creek running under
the old wooden bridge?

What if we do
and find the home place
long gone or in rubble...
the bridge a disgrace?

No, we can't go back,
for nothing's the same;
the family is scattered...
no one is to blame.

The only thing left
is the love we knew there
which we'll keep in the heart
and take everywhere.

Thought for the Day: I know that to live in the past is futile. I shall respect the past but press on, holding in my heart the best of what I remember.

APRIL 19

Scripture Reading: Zephaniah 3:8-13

Verse for the Day: "At the time I will change the speech of the peoples to pure speech..." (Zephaniah 3:9a)

The Monster

Language of the lowest does not signal liberation...
but rather a broad-based educational deterioration.

Ignoble words and acts used as entertainment
inspire insensitive conduct and tragic experiment.

Blasphemy, vulgarity, and obscene attempts at humor
infect the personality as rancid, cancerous tumor.

And if it takes the crude and profane to empower us,
we may find that, once embraced, the monster will
devour us.

Thought for the Day: Today I will not degrade myself or those about me with language crude or profane, nor will I listen to such.

APRIL 20

Scripture Reading: Luke 23:32-43

Verse for the Day: "He replied, 'Truly I tell you, today you will be with me in Paradise.'" (Luke 23:43)

Paradise Today

It's not found in the future
nor in the yesterday;
it's not in lonely brooding
nor frantic fake display.

It's not in binding tension
nor searching wonderment;
it's not found in possessions
nor in monastic bent.

It's not on reigning mountain,
in placid valley stream,
on nature's hearth no matter
how heavenly the dream.

It's found when Christ's assurance
impacts the heart and soul.
Paradise is now when God
alone becomes the goal.

Thought for the Day: I will remember that eternal life begins here and now, and I will aim to live each moment in the promise of paradise today.

APRIL 21

Scripture Reading: John 11:17-44

Verse for the Day: "Jesus began to weep." (John 11:35)

Goodbye

He wanted time to say one last goodbye,
but night's calm let her labored breath abate.
When wakened he would quickly rise and try
to fool himself that it was not too late.

He felt as though his legs would not hold up;
his knees were buckling, and the room went round.
And then, someone was handing him a cup
and leading him outside the hushed compound.

He saw the cars go by as if today
were just like any other day in time.
Did those who drove so fast not see the way
the world was now a reeling paradigm?

For long nights afterwards, he'd turn and toss.
Yet, he knew God's love covered grief and loss.

Thought for the Day: I know there must be some time for grieving, and if today is not the time for me, I will be sensitive to those who are living with sorrow.

APRIL 22

Scripture Reading: Ephesians 5:1-14

Verse for the Day: "Entirely out of place is obscene, silly, and vulgar talk; but instead, let there be thanksgiving." (Ephesians 5:4)

The Little Stream Talks

He yelled across the creek some profane epithet...
then, from the little stream, "How dare you talk like that!"
Startled, he looked aghast and dropped his school lunch box.
He sat down on the bank and started tossing rocks.

"A little creek can't talk," he jeered, then laughed out loud.
"That's what you think!" the stream said, rippling, sun-lit, proud.
"You must not curse or swear or use obscenity,
but be a source of pure refreshment just like me.
I often get so tired of running constantly,
but you don't hear me splash or spout profanity."
As the boy rushed for home, he tripped on fallen limb,
but uttered not a word ... for the creek had talked to him.

Thought for the Day: Sometimes the "better self," which runs deep in each of us, speaks through our fantasies. Today I will listen.

APRIL 23

Scripture Reading: Galatians 6:1-10

Verse for the Day: "Bear one another's burden, and in this way you will fulfill the law of Christ." (Galatians 6:2)

Which Law?

"Help me," she pleaded; the request bounced back,
unregistered, unheeded, with calloused attack...
"No one ever helped me!" the answer was spewed
with venom profusely and with malice imbued.

"Forgive me," he cried... knowing well he deserved
his petition denied and his punishment served.
"My child, you're forgiven." The burden was lifted;
no longer guilt-driven, the emphasis shifted.

The difference here—believe what you will—
is God versus fear. Which law to fulfill?

Thought for the Day: Lord, help me to remember that fulfillment of your law means forgiving, sharing burdens, and loving, even the undeserving.

APRIL 24

Scripture Reading: Romans 12:6-13

Verse for the Day: "Rejoice in hope, be patient in suffering, persevere in prayer." (Romans 12:12)

This is the Day

At daylight he'd arise, stretch tall, and say,
"This is the day the Lord has made. And let
us now rejoice, be glad, and on our way!"
This long-past ritual she can't forget.

And there are other things she still recalls:
his flaming red hair turning silver-gray,
the smiling eyes, the grin which yet enthralls,
as do the words of love she heard each day.

Sometimes it seems the morning's lost its lure;
the out-of-doors they shared seems so forlorn.
Without him she endeavors to endure...
for what cannot be changed is bravely borne.

She knows she'll hear again that cherished voice:
"This is the day the Lord has made... rejoice!"

Thought for the Day: I will remember to give thanks for the opportunities of each day, for the memories of good times shared, and for the anticipation of more to come.

APRIL 25

Scripture Reading: Proverbs 14:26-35

Verse for the Day: "Whoever is slow to anger has great understanding, but one who has a hasty temper exalts folly." (Proverbs 14:29)

That Kind

He was a man whose toes
one dared not step upon.
Quick-tempered, sharp of tongue,
his wild streak was well known.

"He'll end up in some prison,"
they said, with all agreeing,
"just seems to be 'that kind,'
a worthless human being!"

But then, he fell in love;
won a good lady's heart.
She saw in him a man
just needing a new start.

With her help and the Lord's
he put his wild streak behind.
For more than fifty years now
he hasn't been "that kind."

Thought for the Day: Today I'll not judge too harshly, but keep in mind what God can do with a person's future.

APRIL 26

Scripture Reading: Luke 24: 13-35

Verse for the Day: "They said to each other, 'Were not our hearts burning within us while he was talking to us on the road, while he was opening the scriptures to us?'" (Luke 24:32)

Hearts Afire

"Were not our hearts burning within us?"
Sometimes the heart is strangely warmed
by meetings of celestial nature
that leave the ego-driven disarmed.
    To meet God on the road to Emmaus
    or in a prayer at chapel meeting
    can result in stirring passion—
    deep, intense, and not so fleeting.

It doesn't take strategic planning;
one doesn't need a major push;
it may not come as bolt of lightning
nor as a voice from burning bush.
    It may be like the silent sunrise,
    with feather-touch as from a dove
    when heart is melted by the power
    of confrontation with God's love.

Thought for the Day: Confronting God's love in all its depth and intensity is a soul-stirring, life-changing experience.

APRIL 27

Scripture Reading: II Timothy 1:3-14

Verse for the Day: "I am reminded of your sincere faith, a faith that lived first in your grandmother Lois and your mother Eunice and now, I am sure, lives in you." (II Timothy 1:5)

Sincere Faith

My mother's faith is not my own—
our insight's not the same;
I see things very differently.
Should this be cause for shame?

She reads the Scripture literally.
But should the Ghost be blamed
for details there that I perceive
by mortal mind were framed?

Oh, yes, I see the Spirit's hand
throughout the holy pages,
but I must sift the truth myself
through wisdom of the ages.

Though I believe sincerely, Lord,
with awe and trepidation,
I'll place my sincere faith in YOU...
not on interpretation.

Thought for the Day: I'll respect the faith of others but seek God's will through my own experience of the divine.

APRIL 28

Scripture Reading: Romans 12:12-21

Verse for the Day: "Rejoice in hope; be patient in suffering; and persevere in prayer." (Romans 12:12)

Help

Lord, help us to pray rejoicing...
for you know when we're not real.
Keep our hope alive in knowing
you have the power to heal.

Grant healing in whatever way
seems best, and let the light
of your own spirit rest upon
our wounds till all is right.

If suffering is deemed our lot
let patience be companion;
give stamina to stay the course
and strength to span the canyon.

We ask for perseverance in
our attitude toward prayer,
knowing it to be a life line
as essential as fresh air.

Thought for the Day: Today I will persevere in praying that through all circumstances I will find a cause for rejoicing in hope and a strength for patience in suffering.

APRIL 29

Scripture Reading: Matthew 18:1-14

Verse for the Day: "He called a child, whom he put among them, and said, 'Unless you become like children, you will never enter the kingdom of heaven.'" (Matthew 18:2-3)

Through a Child's Eyes

If I could see the world through a child's eyes...
    there would be golden sunshine in blue skies;
    no storms, just gentle rain or pleasant breeze,
    and song birds would be singing in the trees.
If I could see the world through a child's eyes...
    there would be nothing sinister—no lies,
    or wars or enemies or vicious acts
    just backyard swings and peanut butter snacks.
If I could see the world through a child's eyes...
    everyone who's big would also be wise;
    and every little one would be adored,
    and only non-pollutants would be stored.
If I could see the world through a child's eyes...
    every human being would win the prize;
    every trip would end up at Disneyland,
    and everyone could play drums in the band.
If I could see the world through a child's eyes...
    I would not worry about how time flies,
    but rather focus on "just for today"
    then kneel beside my bed and humbly pray.

Thought for the Day: I will remember that 1 must become child-like in acceptance if I would enter the kingdom.

APRIL 30

Scripture Reading: Psalm 6

Verse for the Day: "I am weary with my moaning;" (Psalm 6:6a)

Vacation Time

I may not be able to take a cruise,
but I can give doubting a trip if I choose;
furlough my temper and testiness,
and give my complaining and my distress
a long-needed outing—a holiday.

I may not be able to fly away,
but I'll send my whining and my vexation
on an all-expense paid, prolonged vacation.

I may not be able to travel afar,
but I'll pack my petty, snide words that scar
and critical comments to send on retreat...
and hope they won't find the way back to my street.

Thought for the Day: Today I'll try to be very conscious of the effect my attitude has on those about me, and if needed, I'll "give it a rest."

IT CAME TO PASS

May

MAY 1

Scripture Reading: Ecclesiastes 3:9-15

Verse for the Day: "He has made everything suitable for its time; moreover, he has put a sense of past and future into their minds ..." (Ecclesiastes 3:11a)

Word to the Wise

Treasure the dreams of the future;
savor memories of the past;
hold dear a sense of the present,
but know that it will not last.

Love well the earth and its bounty;
feel pride in the knowledge you gain;
discover the pleasure in beauty,
but know that beauty is vain.

Find time to play and take leisure;
be happy in work that you do;
live well so there'll be no regretting
when time for living is through.

Just know, wherever life takes you,
all comes but to pass in the end;
and LOVE is the only thing lasting,
and GOD is the ultimate friend.

Thought for the Day: If I would make the most of each day, plan for the future, and enjoy thoughts of the past, I must make each decision as if it would be my last.

MAY 2

Scripture Reading: Colossians 3:12-17

Verse for the Day: "... clothe yourselves with compassion, kindness, humility, meekness, and patience ... Above all clothe yourselves with love, which binds everything together in perfect harmony." (Colossians 3:12b,14)

Handle Carefully

The easiest heart of all to break
is the one that truly loves you.
So, handle with care, for heaven's sake,
the heart that's beating true.

Be kind to that one close to you;
strive to be harmonious;
let spiteful pride become taboo
and manners acrimonious.

Speak and act toward the one who loves you
as if that heart were solid gold.
Treat love well worn as if brand new,
for love, so treasured, never grows old.

Thought for the Day: The ones closest to us who truly care about us are the ones to whom we're often most inconsiderate. Today, I resolve that this will not be so.

MAY 3

Scripture Reading: Romans 12:14-21

Verse for the Day: "Rejoice with those who rejoice, weep with those who weep." (Romans 12:15)

When the Weeping Is Done

When I have cried
  with those who are suffering,
and tears have dried,
  let me, remembering,
then seek to make whole
  those who are broken;
to reach the very soul
  of heartache unspoken,
knowing that compassion
  demands more of one
than tears of passion.
  When they are done
the work of healing
  must begin,
thereby revealing
  which of us in
Christ-like manner
  will not stand apart
but carry forth the banner
  and wrap the wounded heart.

Thought for the Day: I will do more than weep for those who are suffering pain or loss; I will reach out in concern.

MAY 4

Scripture Reading: Matthew 12:20-32

Verse for the Day: "Therefore I tell you, people will be forgiven for every sin and blasphemy, but blasphemy against the Spirit will not be forgiven." (Matthew 12:31)

The Unforgivable

We can say "no" so often
to the calling of the Spirit.
that there will come a time too soon
when we'll not even hear it.
The unforgivable is to
refuse to be forgiven.
We won't believe in sin at all
and will not accept a heaven.

Or if we reckon sin as real—
out there among society—
we don't agree that all have sinned—
not if the all includes the me.
When we're inclined to think ourselves
in no need of saving grace,
we need it most of all. For just
the pure in heart will see God's face.

Thought for the Day: I will remember that the only unforgivable sin is to deny oneself forgiveness by denying the need for it; thereby turning away God's spirit

MAY 5

Scripture Reading: Job 12:1-10

Verse for the Day: "But ask the animals, and they will teach you; the birds of the air, and they will tell you; ask the plants of the earth, and they will teach you; and the fish of the sea will declare to you." (Job 12:7-8)

Simple Things

There is peace in simple things:
in the smell of fresh bread;
in the artist's rendering of angel wings;
in the sound, "mama," said
as a baby's first attempted word;
in the phrase "I love you,"
no matter how many times it's heard;
in worship—thoughtful, true.

Whoever finds in these a treasure
will not be overcome
by circumstance, uneven measure
or events that might numb
another. Who cherishes delight
in simple things will find
a reverential calm which—despite
it all—leaves peace of mind.

Thought for the Day: Simplifying our lives in the fashion of animals, birds, fish, and plants, is one lesson they could teach us, as well as reliance on each day's providence.

MAY 6

Scripture Reading: Deuteronomy 26:6-11

Verse for the Day: "You... shall celebrate with all the bounty the Lord your God has given to you and to your house." (Deuteronomy 26:11)

Flowers

On cold, dark days she talks of indoor plants.
She phones with news of blooms on window sill.
Descriptions of bright-colored blossoms fill
our chatting as the winter raves and rants:

pink and purple African violets,
poinsettias which she got at Christmas time
along with lovely cards of Christmas rhyme.
She reads a hundred times each one she gets.

In seasons when the outdoor flowers bloom,
she tells me of the golden daffodils.
The scent of roses from the garden fills
the air, she says, dispelling any gloom.

As one who must spend many hours alone,
she reckons time in terms of flowers grown.

Thought for the Day: I will be more aware of those who live alone, and when I am alone, I'll remember to be thankful for and celebrate the bounty and beauty of God's world.

MAY 7

Scripture Reading: Colossians 1:1-14

Verse for the Day: "May you be strong ... and may you be prepared to endure everything with patience ..." (Colossians 1:11)

Patience

Patience, it's said, is seeing things
from God's point of view.
Endurance comes from knowing that
good shall win in due
time, and vindication will come
to those who pursue
a path of righteousness and peace.

Patience, it's said, is willingness
to believe that time
is on the side of justice. And
even though the crime
rate is sky high, God still sustains
humanity's climb
toward redemption and release.

Thought for the Day: Patience is its own reward. It leaves behind no guilty conscience.

MAY 8

Scripture Reading: Psalm 24

Verse for the Day: "The earth is the Lord's and all that is in it, the world, and those who live in it." (Psalm 24:1)

Agreement

That apple tree spoke to me; it did!
It said its bounty was meant for all.
It asked what right I had in taking
basketfuls in order to forestall
others from coming to share its fruit.
I am afraid I had to admit
that since the apple tree was growing
on my land I figured I owned it.

The tree laughed out loud; I know it did!
Your land? Its tone was quite facetious.
And how, pray tell, did you make this land,
establishing title pretentious?
I tried to explain that while God made
the land, I purchased it properly.
And on what purchase price, the tree asked,
did you and the Creator agree?

Thought for the Day: I will remember that I am only a steward of God's possessions. In everything I am accountable to the Creator for my stewardship.

MAY 9

Scripture Reading: Proverbs 20:12-22

Verse for the Day: "The hearing ear and seeing eye—the Lord has made them both." (Proverbs 20:12)

Sight and Sound

I do not ask for youth to last forever,
but that my eye will never grow so dim
that I will fail to see the pain of others
or overlook the load that's crushing them.
    I would not ask for twenty-twenty vision
    when time and age have taken toll on sight,
    but I do pray for light beyond the seeing
    to comprehend a neighbor's fearful plight.
I do not ask perception of all music
that fills the macrocosmic atmosphere.
but I do hope to hear the sound of crying
if I can ease one dread or dry one tear.
    I would not pass a brother unattended
    if I should hear his calling out to me,
    so I will pray for inner resonating
    of sound that years obscure to some degree.
Oh, Lord, please let me keep the sight and hearing,
when youth and middle age are both long past,
to still discern, because of lifetime habit,
attending ways as long as life shall last.

Thought for the Day: Age should be no barrier to service. As long as possible I will enrich my life by helping others.

MAY 10

Scripture Reading: James 1:5-18

Verse for the Day: "Every generous act of giving, with every perfect gift, is from above, coming down from the Father of lights..." (James l-17a)

It Is Good

I've never fully understood
 why God pronounced all things made "good,"
 if that encompassed likelihood
 that seed of selfish human-kind
 would grow and flourish, so inclined
 to be spoiled rotten, wined and dined;
appalled at thought of sacrifice
 or even being genteel and nice;
 instead, as frigid as block ice—
 suspicious, angry, vengeance bent;
 ungrateful clod, recipient
 of undeserved love, heaven-sent.
Yet, God pronounced "good" what was made
 and put creation in the shade
 of Eden's floral promenade.
 Let's hope the Lord does not despair—
 pronounce "no good" nor even "fair"
 the human being—and cease to care.

Thought for the Day: I rely on God so often, especially when in need of help; why is it, then, that so often God cannot rely on me?

MAY 11

Scripture Reading: Job 37:1-14

Verse for the Day: "... stop and consider the wondrous works of God." (Job 37:14)

Wonders

This morning I awoke and found
      a sheet of ice on frozen ground.
"No use in trying to get through;
      won't be much work done, if I do."
So, I just put my job on hold
      and let myself try to enfold
      the beauty of God's wonderland.
Soon daffodils will start to bloom
      right there beneath that snow-white tomb.
That frost-draped oak will hold a nest
      of redbirds nestled on its chest.
The sleeting winds which hurl ice-breath
      portending signs of nature's death
      will be dispersed by God's own hand.
This world of marvelous delights
      of touch and smell and sound and sight
      is such a cache of natural good
      it ought to bloom in brotherhood.
And will when earth-folk comprehend
      that all are family and friend—
      and all together fall or stand.

Thought for the Day: Today I will share my appreciation for the wonders of the earth and try to live in peace with all.

MAY 12

Scripture Reading: Mark 10:13-16

Verse for the Day: "Truly I tell you, whoever does not receive the kingdom of God as little child will never enter it." (Mark 10:15)

A Child's View of Spring

Spring is when the birds come back;
flowers bloom around the walk,
and Mom is glad when school is out
so she and I can have a talk
about the way the world is made
and how God planned for birds to sing
in old shade trees and flowers bloom
around the walk each happy spring.

I love to climb those old shade trees,
see black-eyed susies watching me,
hear mockingbirds and chickadees
sing ballad of the wild and free.
I like the springtime best of all,
and I think God is glad to be
the cause of birds and flowers and trees
and springtime talks for Mom and me.

Thought for the Day: I know that little children are filled with wonder and appreciation for the simplest things. I, too, will be more appreciative.

MAY 13

Scripture Reading: Luke 15:11-32

Verse for the Day: "Now his elder son was in the field; and when he came and approached the house, he heard music and dancing... Then he became angry and refused to go in." (Luke 15:25,28)

The Prodigal

I have loved the Bible story all about the prodigal son;
and I am here to tell you I can spot them, every one.
With their youth and treasure wasted and their wild oats
     harvested,
they are more than ready to return to home's good food and
     bed.
And there's nothing more disquieting than to see a parent's
     arm
open quickly to enfold them just as if they'd meant no
     harm.
While the one who stayed and labored in the home fields
     all the while
never got a single thing beyond a handshake and a smile.
Now, don't tell me I'm mistaken, that it reads a
     different way.
The elder son ... a prodigal? The heck you say!
That he wasted opportunity on envy of the other...?
That's the one I never recognized. I am the elder brother.

Thought for the Day: Envy is just as alienating a force as distance, perhaps even more so.

MAY 14

Scripture Reading: Psalm 9:1-8

Verse for the Day: "I will give thanks to the Lord with my whole heart; ... I will be glad and exult in you; I will sing praise to your name, O Most High." (Psalm 9: la,2)

Real Prayer

> It doesn't do much good to pray
> if we act like crusty clumps of clay;
> the soured countenance of a clod
> is a cloud across the face of God.
>
> It doesn't do much good to pray
> if it doesn't brighten someone's way;
> the grumpy head that fails to nod
> turns down its chance of greeting God.
>
> The prayer that recognizes grace
> puts a smile of joy upon the face,
> and power grows in the fertile sod
> of the prayerful heart which smiles with God.

Thought for the Day: A smile is the universal language, and, like a battery, an ever-ready smile just keeps the joy in life going, and going, and going.

MAY 15

Scripture Reading: I John 4:7-16

Verse for the Day: "... for God is love." (I John 4:8b)

Questions

A struggling young student once asked
a very wise man to explain,
why, if there's God, in infinite power,
there is also suffering and pain.
He questioned all matters of faith,
but would live by the Golden Rule.
Instead of God, only goodness
would be his creed and his school.
"Goodness," he said, "I will live by.
Now, tell me, sir, if you can,
what is wrong with worshiping only
what I can understand?"
"My friend, you've forgotten something,"
the wise man answered the youth.
"**Good** is the most mysterious thing
in the boundless maze of truth.
And no one can understand it,
as mysteries are prod,
and no one can explain it
apart from a living God."

Thought for the Day: I know that God is love and love is good, therefore, God is good. Love or good cannot be explained apart from God.

MAY 16

Scripture Reading: Proverbs 4:10-18

Verse for the Day: "But the path of the righteous is like the light of dawn, which shines brighter and brighter until full day." (Proverbs 4:18)

For Ninety Years

For ninety years she relished each day's dawn,
no matter what condition of the sky.
She'd fire the wash tub, scrub clothes, hang them on
the line when clear, mild weather proved ally.

But if storm clouds had brushed the sun aside
and winds whipped pelting rain like sheets, instead,
she'd set to baking pies and take in stride
the inside chores which on clear days she'd dread.

For she did love the out-of-doors, and while
she washed and ironed for folks, she'd sometimes rest
a spell out on the porch to wave and smile
at kids from school reciting rhymes in jest.

Her last dawn's greeting now has come and gone.
At ninety-one she peacefully passed on.

Thought for the Day: The way we greet the day often tells what kind of persons we are. I resolve to begin waking up with more enthusiasm for the day at hand.

MAY 17

Scripture Reading: Psalm 136:1-7

Verse for the Day: "O give thanks to the Lord, for he is good, for his steadfast love endures forever." (Psalm 136:1)

God's Steadfast Love

God's love shines forth in everything we see
if love of God is what we're looking for.
The violent storm that wrecks community
brings loads of goodwill in from every shore.

The child who's trapped and must be urgently
attended if she can be saved at all
is uppermost on every mind till she
gets free and safe within hospital wall.

The multi-car pile-up that shatters time
arouses instinct of the good Samaritan.
A thousand tears are shed with every chime
of church bell when the funeral is done.

God's love shines forth in everything we see
if love of God shines forth from you and me.

Thought for the Day: If I believe a better world begins with me and that God is at the center of that better world, then I must do all I can to spread the word that God is Love.

MAY 18

Scripture Reading: Isaiah 6

Verse for the Day: "Then I heard the voice of the Lord saying, 'Whom shall I send, and who will go for us?' And I said, 'Here am I, send me!'" (Isaiah 6:8)

Involvement

I do not want to run from involvement,
    to hide behind "too busy" or "too tired,"
    to plead that someone else needs to be sent—
    someone more talented or more inspired.
To say that I'm not able just to hold
    a dampened cloth against a fevered brow
    or rock a lonely child or to enfold
    an aging friend shelved by the system now...
    would be to crucify my faith that God
    can move a mountain—even one like me.
So much gets done by those who simply plod
    along the path of daily charity.

Although my feeble efforts won't provide
    the remedy, let it be said, I tried.

Thought for the Day: I will not try to escape my responsibility to be involved with the world's problems and hopefully a part of the solution.

MAY 19

Scripture Reading: Genesis 21:1-7

Verse for the Day: "God has brought laughter for me; everyone who hears will laugh with me." (Genesis 21:6b)

When Sarah Laughed

When Sarah laughed ... such laughter,
for she could not keep quiet.
God's message through an angel
brought word she thought not right.

Impossible! she reasoned,
but nothing she had heard
was beyond the possible
if God had spoke the word.

And lo, behold, in old age,
she bore Abram a son.
Her laughter, then, was joyous,
and shared by everyone.

To ridicule as folly
God-inspired intention
is reckless disregard of
the divine dimension.

Thought for the Day: It's best not to scoff at the idea of a miracle, and today I will be open to all possibilities where God is concerned.

MAY 20

Scripture Reading: Matthew 21:18-22

Verse for the Day: "Whatever you ask for in prayer with faith, you will receive." (Matthew 21:22)

We Pray

We offer praise, Lord, for your constant care,
acknowledging our need and our dependence.
Please bless this day you've given us to share
the measure of your bounty and your prudence.

Remind us as we try to make it through
whatever test or trial we might be meeting
that you have vital work for us to do,
and time is ever passing—oh, so fleeting.

Please keep before us always those in need—
our hearts and minds in focus on a mission—
that what we are in thought and word and deed
will be of your divine intent fruition.

We offer thanks, Lord, for each answered prayer,
and for the urge to pray that proves you're there.

Thought for the Day: When I feel led to pray, moved to communicate with God, that, in itself, is evidence of God's presence, for which I am thankful.

MAY 2I

Scripture Reading: I Corinthians 13:8-13

Verse for the Day: "Now faith, hope, and love aide, but the greatest of these is love." (I Corinthians 13:13)

Remembered Love

Each day of life I know I'm building
memory blocks to walk upon
when day is past and there is neither
time nor strength—for all is gone,
except the blocks on which to walk
and smell the flowers by the way.
I'll cherish in the mind's recesses
times when sunshine's golden ray
covered day with beams of blessing,
making strong those memory blocks
leading through hereafter's portals
which remembered love unlocks.

Thought for the Day: I will remember that the time may come when only memory is left, and only the memory of love will be worth remembering.

MAY 22

Scripture Reading: 2 Peter 1:1-11

Verse for the Day: "... you must make every effort to support your faith with goodness, and goodness with knowledge ..." (2 Peter 1:5)

The Truth Is ...

"The truth is ..." we have all heard someone say,
and then commence to make known holy writ.
Were truth (and truth alone) our resume,
veracity (unvouched) a requisite ...
then goodness of such faithful would make clear
that what proceeds from mouth as truth would be,
in fact, legitimate; would not appear
to need a preface of validity.
It's good to know the truth when it is heard,
and it's been said the truth will make us free,
but "truth" which follows statement of that word
suggests an unfamiliarity.
   Possession of real virtue makes uncouth
   the need to say, "I'm telling you the truth."

Thought for the Day: I will remember that truth is its own authentication and that knowledge which proceeds from faith and goodness can stand on its own merit.

MAY 23

Scripture Reading: Revelation 3:15-22

Verse for the Day: "Listen! I am standing at the door, knocking; if you hear my voice and open the door, I will come in to you and eat with you and you with me." (Revelation 3:20)

The Knock

To doubters all
>who hear the call...
God waits outside;
>so open wide
the heart's locked door;
>there's so much more
than you have known
>or earth has shown.

God's mercy shared;
>love's might unspared;
grace not restrained;
>peace unexplained.
Lost hope now found
>on faith's high ground.
Assurance, too,
>that God loves you.

Thought for the Day: Today I will listen for God's knock at my heart's door, and answering. I will make the Lord welcome in my life.

MAY 24

Scripture Reading: Proverbs 12:1-16

Verse for the Day: "The words of the wicked are a deadly ambush, but the speech of the upright delivers them." (Proverbs 12:6)

A Good Word

He never hesitates to say a word
    of kindness to another,
to praise a child or lift the spirit of
    a broken-hearted brother.

While some may let a friend's anxiety
    abide, he will make mention,
take notice, and ask if he can be of help.
    He always pays attention.

A word, a smile, a hand, a shoulder broad
    and sturdy to lean upon.
He is a gentle man, a very good
    listener, sometimes 'til dawn

a troubled neighbor will take advantage
    of his kind-hearted patience;
sit and talk the night away through specters
    of grief or pangs of conscience.

With "What's the good word?" he will greet a friend.
    And to his list of those there is no end.

Thought for the Day: There are many people to whom a good word or a listening ear is all it would take to brighten their day. I will not hesitate to offer both.

MAY 25

Scripture Reading: I John 3:18-24

Verse for the Day: "Little children, let us love not in word or speech, but in truth and action." (I John 3:18)

God's Love Abides

It's wonderful to love the sky,
the out-of-doors, the birds which fly,
but love of nature will not do
when there's a brother needing you.

To keep a spotless house is nice,
but cleanliness will not suffice
when there are those with no abode
who need someone to share their load.

The love of family should lead
to broad concern for those in need,
for it should not be hard to see
that humankind's a family.

God's love abides in only those
who care for all—who don't suppose
they're better 'cause they have the most.
They know they're guests—God is the host.

Thought for the Day: Sharing is the only real demonstration of caring. I will not begrudge any request for help and will be generous in response.

158

MAY 26

Scripture Reading: Matthew 25:31-46

Verse for the Day: "Truly I tell you, just as you did it to one of the least of these who are members of my family, you did it to me." (Matthew 25:40)

Hunger

Where hunger hurts
let me not rest content
until all efforts
at relief are spent...
until I've looked
into its hollow eyes
and felt the death-grip
silence can't disguise
and, in that feeling recognized
the brotherhood,
the sisterhood,
the childhood
we all share,
the family ties
reminding us who care
that life
is brief,
and only in communion
is relief.

Thought for the Day: I want to be more sensitive to the world-wide problem of hunger. Today I will become better informed and more responsive.

MAY 27

Scripture Reading: Ecclesiastes 3:20-26

Verse for the Day: "For the one who pleases him God gives wisdom and knowledge and joy." (Ecclesiastes 3:26a)

My Scenario

> The tree looked so inviting,
>   shading spot for reverie;
> I plopped on grassy pallet,
>   leaned back and failed to see
> the poison ivy vine
>   which cradled me.
> Spent awhile just thinking
>   wishing for the time
> to sort out all the conflicts,
>   to find in life a rhyme
> and reason for it all.
>   I dreamed I might design
> a scenario for living—
>   a lifetime script in which
> Murphy's Law did not apply,
>   the proverbial stitch
> in time was always made,
>   and poison ivy did not itch.

Thought for the Day: Life is short, and there are times of distress and weeping. But good humor and laughter are also meant to be a vital part of life.

MAY 28

Scripture Reading: John 10:1-18

Verse for the Day: "I am the good shepherd; I know my own and my own know me." (John 10:15)

The Shepherd

If we have asked the Lord to lead us
then there's no need for all the fuss.
We fume and frustrate in a whir,
as if, by fate, doomed to incur
wrath of nature, mankind, and beast.

God's promise of care for the least
of earth's children—a steadfast wing
of divine undergirding—
is ours for accepting. And whether
in life or death, alone or together,
through whatever circumstance or state,
the Spirit will be with us—innate
and dynamic—as friend and guide
until we move to the other side.

As shepherd to sheep, our Lord remains
ever the Savior whose love sustains.

Thought for the Day: I will pray that the shepherding love and care God promises will be a steadfast surety in my mind so that worry will not overwhelm me.

MAY 29

Scripture Reading: Psalm 37:34-40

Verse for the Day: "Wait for the Lord, and keep to his way ..." (Psalm 37:34a)

Without a Doubt

There is a hymn which says, "Be still my soul,"
the Lord is on your side." To comprehend
this fact in my heart is my one goal.
I want to know my Creator as friend.

So awesome is the term "Creator" that
I want to know such force is on my side,
that when my dreams are shattered, hopes fall flat,
I can, with dignity, take it in stride ...

Assured that waiting will not be in vain;
that there is nothing God and I cannot
resolve successfully and use for gain.
No matter when or where ... no matter what!

"Be still my soul, the Lord is on your side"
is all about a "peace" the world cannot provide.

Thought for the Day: I will pray devoutly, routinely, and often, and then rely on God to shepherd me through whatever in life is my lot.

MAY 30

Scripture Reading: Mark 6:44-56

Verse for the Day: "When evening came, the boat was out on the sea, and he was alone on the land." (Mark 6:47)

The Woods

When I've spent days or weeks
　　　away from the land,
my famished spirit seeks
　　　that tall, stately stand
of oak and elm and pine
　　　which I call "the woods."
It's canopy enshrines
　　　the wild neighborhood;
makes a sanctuary
　　　where hymn-singing leaves
and wind chants confirm me.
　　　Yakking squirrel believes
his sermonizing will
　　　lead me to agree
I don't belong here. Still,
　　　I remain to see
the sun's benediction
　　　with new conviction.

Thought for the Day: Time spent alone for meditation and prayer is essential to a healthy spirit, and I must schedule such time each day.

MAY 31

Scripture Reading: Proverbs 19:11-27

Verse for the Day: "Cease straying my child from the words of knowledge in order that you may hear instruction." (Proverbs 19:27)

Today

Today I want to be more loving.
      but temper rears its ugly head.
Today I want to help somebody,
      but self remains supreme instead.

Today, I want to be more patient,
      but "hurry" is my middle name.
Today I would be understanding,
      but still I'm quick to apportion blame.

Today I want to be more trusting,
      but cynicism holds me back ...
Today I would be generous,
      but charity's not been my knack.

Oh, Lord, I know the path to failure
      is paved with good intentions meant,
and yesterday will haunt forever
      if today is unwisely spent.

Thought for the Day: Today I resolve to be more loving, helpful, patient, understanding, trusting, and generous.

CARRYING LIGHT

June

JUNE 1

Scripture Reading: Matthew 5:13-20

Verse for the Day: "... let your light shine before others so that they may see your good works and give glory to your Father in heaven."
(Matthew 5:16)

He Carried Light

We keep oil lamps for use when lights go out
as they do often during storms,
    and sometimes when
    we sit within
the glow of lamplight my heart warms
to memories of oil lamps all about
my granddad's house as evening spread throughout.
I see my granddad still with lamp in hand
as he would head for bed, and say, "I'll see
    you at daylight."
    And he was right.
He'd get up with the chickens and wake me
to go with him to milk. I'd just go stand
and watch the ritual as sun rose on the land.
I always wished to keep Granddad in sight
for just to be around him made
    me feel secure.
    I thought for sure
that with him I would never be afraid.
I always knew my granddad carried light,
for his presence made my summer visits bright.

Thought for the Day: "Let your light shine." Simple but difficult. To be a carrier of light takes effort.

JUNE 2

Scripture Reading: Ephesians 4:25-31

Verse for the Day: "Put away from you all bitterness and wrath and anger and wrangling and slander, together with all malice, and be kind to one another, tenderhearted forgiving one another, as God in Christ has forgiven you." (Ephesians 4:31)

My Soul to Take

Whenever malice lives in me,
I miss the deep
contentment guiltless conscience brings
and restful sleep.

Whenever I let jealousy
control my mind,
its grip confines me to despair—
no peace I find.

Lord, let all bitterness and wrath
depart from me,
and let me treasure kindness, lest
I fail to see ...

that charity in thought and speech
is for my sake,
if I would have a soul fit for
the Lord to take.

Thought for the Day: The child's prayer, "If I should die before I wake, I pray Thee, Lord, my soul to take," provides adults with food for thought.

JUNE 3

Scripture Reading: Luke 10:30-37

Verse for the Day: "A man was going down from Jerusalem to Jericho, and fell into the hand of robbers who stripped him, beat him, and went away leaving him half dead. ... a Samaritan, while traveling came near him, and when he saw him, he was moved to pity ... and took care of him." (Luke 10: 30b, 33, 34b)

Unto Others

She dresses in tatters and wanders the streets;
she's cordial and caring toward each one she meets.
To homeless young children she hands out balloons;
if anyone's hurt she nurses the wounds.
She shares food she's brought, and sometimes she tries
to talk alcoholics, who live on their lies,
into a shelter to find some relief.
She shifts through the refuge of desperate grief.
She listens to stories that bring her to tears
and senses the dreading as darkness nears.
She gives out the blankets she's stored in her cart,
then calls it a day, and, leaving her heart,
gets into a taxi, heads home for the night,
and feels pangs of conscience at the opulent sight
of her smart neighborhood, so safe and so neat.
So tomorrow will find her back on the street.

Thought for the Day: Each day usually presents an opportunity to be of service to someone in need; if not, I can choose to create the opportunity.

JUNE 4

Scripture Reading: Ecclesiastes 11

Verse for the Day: "Send out your bread upon the waters, for after many days you will get it back." (Ecclesiastes 11:1)

Stale Bread?

Perhaps he was too tired
or uninspired,
but pleas for a good word
all went unheard.
They did not ask for much—
a caring touch.
A father's love they sought;
tough talk he brought.
Now he is old, alone
and looks upon
his children for support,
but they just resort
to justification
of deeds undone
by saying if they could
they surely would.
But still, now that they're grown,
he's left alone.

Thought for the Day: I would remember that bread cast upon the water can be stale bread, and that, too, will return. I must make sure that the bread I cast is lovingly cast and fresh.

JUNE 5

Scripture Reading: Isaiah 46:1-4

Verse for the Day: "I have made, and I will bear; I will carry and will save." (Isaiah 46:4a)

In Heroic Mode

He is one of the world's good people;
a runner with wings on his feet;
as sure-eyed as the soaring eagle—
as genuine as ever you'd meet.

Not everyone can be a runner;
nor can each have vision precise.
But all of us can be "good people,"
unaffected and just plain "nice."

The wind beneath the wings of eagles
is that same force that carries all
of us who trust in God's upholding
to make the race a winning call.

God's promise means that Holy Will
is to forever replenish
the sight we need to find the pathway,
stay the course, and finally finish.

Thought for the Day: It's great to have, as a hero, one who is as "good" as he or she is gifted. The world needs more heros whose gift it is to run (or walk) with the Lord.

JUNE 6

Scripture Reading: Matthew 19:1-15

Verse for the Day: "... Jesus said, 'Let the little children come to me, and do not stop them; for it is to such as these that the kingdom of heaven belongs.'" (Matthew 19:14)

For a Son

I pray that he will love
the flower and the tree;
that he will recognize
the beauty of the sea.

I pray that he will find
real joy in butterflies;
that he will realize
there's art in apple pies.

I pray that he will keep
the satisfaction of
delight in simple things
like family and love.

I pray that he will stay
child-like in innocence,
but grow up strong and sure,
unshaken by events.

I pray that he will be
true to the best he knows—
ever closer to God
the farther from home he goes.

Thought for the Day: Parents who wish only the best for their growing children will remember always to pray that they will grow closer to God.

JUNE 7

Scripture Reading: Luke 12:16-21

Verse for the Day: "I will pull down my barns and build larger ones, and there I will store all my grain and my goods." (Luke 12:18b)

Things

Those "Carport Sale"
signs never fail
to catch my eye.

A person's junk
I can't debunk,
for it is my

treasure. And it's
never call quits
until I spy

that perfect "thing"
to buy. I bring
it home and try

to find its spot...
then wonder what
on earth? And why?

Thought for the Day: So many possessions are not essential. And often I buy things I don't even have a place for. I resolve to be more discerning.

JUNE 8

Scripture Reading: Proverbs 29:1-7

Verse for the Day: "The righteous know the rights of the poor; the wicked have no such understanding." (Proverbs 29:7)

Remembered

"He's a hard man,"
  they would say,
as if to explain
  his stingy way.
His grave, unmarked,
  is overgrown;
it's somewhere near
  the road, alone.

His neighbor, Mabel
  Reed, was known
though widowed young
  and all alone,
as generous even
  to a fault;
an angel graces
  her burial vault.

Thought for the Day: If I wish to be remembered as warm-hearted and generous, I must practice generosity every day.

JUNE 9

Scripture Reading: Matthew 25:14-30

Verse for the Day: "... I was afraid, and I went and hid your talent in the ground. Here you have what is yours." (Matthew 25:25b)

Is It I?

I can imagine what the fellow felt
who hid his one, lone talent in the ground.
He lost it just because he was afraid
and wanted to preserve it safe and sound.

I'll bet that somewhere back along the way
he shared a talent with someone he cared
about and was rebuffed or ridiculed.
From that time on I'll bet he never dared.

Still, he will be forgiven, even though
he'll have to bear the meted punishment
of forfeiting his talent through neglect
and suffering the censor that was sent.

But, I don't know about the other one—
the one who laughed or mocked the early try;
that one may face a sorely dire fate.
Oh, Lord, I only hope it wasn't I.

Thought for the Day: There is no excuse for harshness or thoughtlessness which leaves anyone feeling less worthy or unloved. To be thoughtful of another's feelings is the least I can do.

JUNE 10

Scripture Reading: Matthew 5:43-48

Verse for the Day: "But I say to you, love your enemies and pray for those who persecute you ..." (Matthew 5:44)

My Enemy and Me

I wither in the face
of animosity.
Is there a way to truly
love the enemy?

Is it the Lord's demand
that I always conform,
accepted only if I
dutifully perform?

Why, then, must I respond
as others think I should?
Why should my opposite
deny my personhood?

And yet, I know that I
must pray for those who rile
or ridicule or harm ...
must go the second mile.

Still, I believe that peace
doesn't mean conformity,
and God loves us as we are—
my enemy and me.

Thought for the Day: It is hard to love one's enemies ... possible only when I remember that God loves both of us.

JUNE 11

Scripture Reading: Proverbs 17:14-24

Verse for the Day: "A friend loves at all times..." (Proverbs 17:17a)

Worth the Risk?

I'd like a special friend for me,
one who is steadfast—one who'd see
that I have faults but would agree
that they were not what made me "me."

One friend who'd stand by, come what may,
to laugh and cry with, work and play,
to share a summer holiday
or just a shopping get-away.

Yet, I'm aware that all depends
on how much "me" I will expend,
when cost of friendship never ends
and has indefinite dividends.

That special one I'd find somewhere
is out there now and needs to share
my friendship and to know I care.
But it is risky. Do I dare?

Thought for the Day: Friendship cannot be maintained with a manipulative attitude? "What's in it for me?" won't sustain a relationship, for the dividends from friendship are uncertain at best.

JUNE 12

Scripture Reading: Psalm 15

Verse for the Day: "Oh, Lord, who may abide in your tent? Who may dwell on your holy hill? Those who walk blamelessly and do what is right, and speak the truth from their heart." (Psalm 15:1,2)

The Handshake

I like to see men shake hands;
it seems brotherly, and when
they meet with a warm handshake
and part with another, then
one can be almost certain
that what went on between
was not animosity.
Even strangers who are seen
shaking hands are perceived
as friendly sorts. I believe
small children should be taught
to shake hands. It's cause to grieve
when manners are not instilled.
The act of shaking hands
is a gentle, gracious deed
that places no demands
on either except truthful
civility. And a bit
of that goes a long way in
this world so in need of it.

Thought for the Day: Hand-shaking, said to be a prehistoric gesture, indicated that the extended hand held no weapon. Its significance today is nonetheless important.

JUNE 13

Scripture Reading: Romans 2:1-11

Verse for the Day: "Therefore, you have no excuse, whoever you are, when you judge others; for in passing judgment on another you condemn yourself..." (Romans 1:1a)

The Reason

She bickered, oh my, how she loved to!
She gossiped and roused deep suspicion.
Her mean-spirit somehow would surface
even when not her main mission.

She looked for the worst in each person;
seemed driven to ferment a turmoil.
She tried to drive wedges of rancor
between friends who had always been loyal.

She never did marry; no wonder!
And as she grew old kids would whisper.
"There's old Miss Miranda, you better
watch out 'cause the devil lives in 'er."

It was after her death that we found out
from a brother, himself a recluse,
that old Miss Miranda through childhood
was subjected to brutish abuse.

Thought for the Day: An old proverb says, "If you understand the reason, you can forgive anything." Many times it's easier not to know the "why."

JUNE 14

Scripture Reading: Psalm 115:12-18

Verse for the Day: "The heavens are the Lord's heavens, but the earth he has given to human beings." (Psalm 115:16)

What Price?

What price can be put on a sunset
    over Yosemite National Park
or on a view from the Empire State Building
    when the lights come on at dark?
What price can be put on the moment
    Niagara Falls comes into view
or on the thrill evoked by a trip
    down the Colorado in a canoe?
What price should we put on the majesty
    of Grand Canyon's multiple hues
or on the awesome wonder evoked
    through Redwood Forest avenues?
Who could price the Painted Desert's
    braided, multi-colored tapestry,
or hang a price tag on stalactites
    and stalagmites of Mammoth artistry.
What price the sunshine on October
    tones in Rockies, Ozarks, Appalachians
or on the special spectacle of
    New England's autumn coronation?
There is no rate of exchange to cover
    the bountiful beauty God has in store.
Gifts without price are all around us;
    how could we ask for anything more?

Thought for the Day: Today I will look for the beauty beyond price all around me. I need to develop the appreciation for that which has no price tag attached.

JUNE 15

Scripture Reading: Matthew 24:32-51

Verse for the Day: "Heaven and earth will pass away; but my word will not pass away." (Matthew 24:35)

A Word

There's nothing else in all the world
as lovely as a word.
As gorgeous as a sunset is
or radiant redbird,
yet still the word of kindness ranks
as beauty unsurpassed.
For though I marvel at the sight
of snow, it will not last,
and while a tree in autumn shades
of red and burnished gold
with sunlight playing on the leaves
is something to behold,
there is nothing so exquisite
as just the one right word
spoken at the one right moment
it needed to be heard.

Thought for the Day: Words are so powerful, and I would aim always to use them wisely. I am thankful for beautiful words fitly spoken and for God's word which will never fail.

JUNE 16

Scripture Reading: II Timothy 2:20-26

Verse for the Day: "Have nothing to do with stupid and senseless controversies; you know that they breed quarrels." (II Timothy 2:23)

A Better Way

He shys from steamy controversy
or confrontation and, oh mercy
how he abhors the hint of a fight.
Always has. As a child he took flight
when trouble approached and never went
looking for it. He acquired a bent
for diplomacy, compromise, tact.
He became an attorney, in fact,
and thinks the only way to succeed
(in contrast to a number of his breed)
is to settle out-of-court. And he
seems adept at that. The tendency
to negotiate is his forte.
He always finds it easy to say—
with diligence, honesty, insight—
"Let's work at this—work—instead of fight!"

Thought for the Day: It takes real strength of character to be a peace maker. When the first inclination is attack, there is great credit in being willing to work things out instead of fighting.

JUNE 17

Scripture Reading: Psalm 141

Verse for the Day: "Set a guard over my mouth, O Lord; keep watch over the door of my lips." (Psalm 141:3)

To Speak or Not to Speak

Oh Lord, set a guard on my mouth;
keep watch at the door of my lips.
You know, Lord, how very often
some unworthy clatter just slips
right by in moments of weakness.

I try not to speak without thought;
I want to be disciplined in
anger, not unduly distraught.
I want to be kindly spoken,
but time and again I have tripped.
If ugly words stuck to my mouth,
I'd be most obsenely fat-lipped.

I try to control my temper;
to anchor my will to your ways,
but somehow when I am tested
my big mouth forgets and soon strays.

So, Lord, set a guard on my mouth,
and bridle my tongue with reserve.
Let only those words pass my lips
which might lift or comfort or serve.

Thought for the Day: There is a discipline involved in using words only in a positive way, and it takes a constant communion with God to develop it.

JUNE 18

Scripture Reading: Luke 6:20-31

Verse for the Day: "Do to others as you would have them do to you; for this is the law and the prophets." (Luke 6:31)

Respect

"Leave the woodpile a little higher
than you found it," he often said;
"You get back your mete as your measure."
He was always thinking ahead.

Not living outside of the present
but consciously being aware
that today determines the future,
so today must be lived with care.

He routinely visited nursing homes.
His own parents were long deceased,
so those living there became his own,
and he grieved when their ills increased.

He thought "respect" was what was missing
from age that made the soul depressed.
His life's goal was to provide it, and
in so doing his own life was blessed.

Thought for the Day: The Golden Rule became "golden" because its value has been proven time and time again.

JUNE 19

Scripture Reading: Romans 14:12-23

Verse for the Day: "Let us therefore no longer pass judgment on one another, but resolve instead never to put a stumbling block or hinderance in the way of another." (Romans 14:13)

To a Different Drum

She stooped, turned on the lamp,
which she kept on the sill,
and whispered to herself,
"I guess I always will,
Jim, until you come home."
>The last time she had heard
from him he was in Nome,
Alaska—he had called
collect to let her know
that he was still alive.
A wanderer, he had
been gone from home for five
long years. A mother's heart
keeps track of every day.
>At night she left the lamp
on just in case. She'd say,
I just can't understand
his constant need to roam,
but, "Jim, you'll always find
the light left on at home."
She really never knew
quite what to make of him.
So every night she prays,
"God, please look after Jim."

Thought for the Day: To those who march in step with a drum beat I do not hear, I want to be patient and understanding.

JUNE 20

Scripture Reading: Romans 15:5-13

Verse for the Day: "May the God of steadfastness and encouragement grant you to live in harmony with one another." (Romans 15:5a)

In Harmony

I want to live in harmony with my neighbors;
to share a word of kindness and concern;
to spend time in the early evening out-of-doors
and visit with the strollers who pass by; to learn
what's going on within their homes and families.
I take some fresh-baked cookies to the couple 'cross
the street and sit with them while they share memories.
I always fix a casserole when there's a loss.

If I can be a friend each day or do some good ...
If I can meet some need another might not see,
I'll live in harmony within my neighborhood.
What's more, I'll live in harmony within me!

Thought for the Day: Harmony, like peace, begins within; I must seek to create harmony if I would live harmoniously with myself and all others.

JUNE 21

Scripture Reading: John 15:9-17

Verse for the Day: "No one has greater love than this, to lay down one's life for one's friends." (John 15:13)

A Friend in Need

The greatest thing
when I'm feeling blue
and I've no sunshine to lend
is to see some
freely offered
in the genuine smile of a friend.

When the time comes
that I'm tossed about
and ready to break in the bend,
it's great to find hope
re-emerging
with the extended hand of a friend.

Most precious of all
when life is shattered
and things don't seem to mend
is the steadfast
reassurance
that I can still count on my friend.

Thought for the Day: Friendship is not something to take for granted ... but something I must nourish and tend, be willing to sacrifice for, and for which to be deeply grateful.

JUNE 22

Scripture Reading: James 3:13-18

Verse for the Day: "Show by your good life that your works are done with gentleness born of wisdom." (James 3:13)

Gentleness Born of Wisdom

"Gentleness born of wisdom" will not be
the morning's headline in the newspaper.
Oh, never would the editors agree
that such would define the sort of caper
which would capture the readers' attention
and crystalize the public's fancy for
the scandalous. It goes without mention
that good news is considered such a bore.

So, if it's notoriety you crave—
to see your name in print or on TV,
your gentleness may not be all the rave,
your good works nothing anyone will see.

But still, if gentle wisdom's what you choose,
that's headline stuff in heaven's daily news.

Thought for the Day: The behind-the-scenes deeds of goodness and gentleness born of wisdom (of which we are all capable) are what holds the fabric of society together.

JUNE 23

Scripture Reading: III John 9-15

Verse for the Day: "Beloved, do not imitate what is evil, but imitate what is good." (III John 11a)

Inspiration in Reverse

She knew the power of words
and used them like a fist,
never sparing anyone,
unable to resist

a dig or sharp retort.
She bristled like a cat,
with back arched and claws bared,
and grew to look like that.

Spurning civility,
she meant to aggravate ...
fed on animosity
and fanned the flames of hate.

We all felt sorry for
the one who drew her wrath
and tried to keep ourselves
out of her vengeful path.

She was devoid of grace—
an inspiration in reverse!
We tried not to be like her ...
thinking nothing could be worse!

Thought for the Day: I will remember to think before I speak today so that anyone listening will not have reason to regret the encounter.

JUNE 24

Scripture Reading: Acts 3:1-16

Verse for the Day: "... I have no silver or gold; but what I have I give you..." (Acts 3:6a)

Words That I Could See

You did not give me a heart-shaped
    box of soft-centered chocolates,
but you replaced the towel-draped
    cupboard door with glass so my plates,
outlined with ornate gold framing,
    could be seen by all. You did not
give me a dozen red roses with card naming
    me your "one and only," and what
is more ... you did not give me
    the silver and gold watch I spotted
in the display case and took you to see.
    But you did revive my potted
plants by re-potting and fertilizing,
    and you did build a fence that's wide
across the yard so my dogs—Bing,
    and Perry, and Frank—could play outside.
You did not get me a gift, it's true,
    but you did take my car to be
serviced, and you said, as you always do,
    "I love you," in words that I could see.

Thought for the Day: Sometimes the nicest way to say "I love you" is by doing something kind for another. A helpful act may say more than many words or gifts.

JUNE 25

Scripture Reading: Mark 4:35-41

Verse for the Day: "He woke up and rebuked the wind, said to the sea, 'Peace! Be still!' Then the wind ceased, and there was a dead calm." (Mark 4:39)

In the Boat

When waves of disappointment jeopardize
my sail through life's uncharted waterways
I must remember waves will not capsize
the boat whose captain's will and word still stays
the wind. When storm-proportion gales of grief
imperil journey on the sea of life,
the master of the deep provides relief
and soothes the raging zephyr that runs rife.
When hail of trouble threatens my small skiff
and billows of distress engage to sink
the vessel I must travel in, and if
the craft should toss and teeter on the brink,
I will remain assured that it will float
as long as God is with me in the boat.

Thought for the Day: No matter what adversities I should encounter today or hereafter, I will be O.K. if I remember that an all-powerful God is always with me.

JUNE 26

Scripture Reading: Isaiah 32: 14-18

Verse for the Day: "My people will abide in a peaceful habitation, in secure dwellings, and in quiet resting places." (Isaiah 32:18)

This Old House

If this old house could talk ...
he'd say as he wandered through
from room to room of scarred
and withered boards in effort to
determine if anything there was
worth the salvage trouble and cost.
He hated to tear down the past
for he knew something dear was lost
each time one of these old homes
was razed to make room for the new.

He often said that he could tell,
by sense of aura as he walked through,
if those who lived there long ago
had been happy and secure within,
if peace was shared by habitants,
or if turmoil and rancor had been
the order of the day. The walls,
he said, bore witness, and the floors.
If this old house could talk ...
he'd say, as he carefully shut the doors.

Thought for the Day: I wonder what my house would say about me. Today I will say and do only those things which would bear repeating.

JUNE 27

Scripture Reading: Psalm 119:162-176

Verse for the Day: "Great peace have those who love your law, nothing can make them stumble." (Psalm 119:165)

Sure Enough

That little robin never knew
the window glass he tried to go through
was double thick and meant to last.
Alas, his effort to bombast
it left no scratch or crack but just
the little robin all a-bust.

To butt one's head against a brick
proves nothing but the head is thick
and leaves a headache which won't quit,
eyes that won't focus, brains a-twit.
It's better to concede that when
defying nature you can't win.

The little robin should have flown
on a course that was well-known.
And human beings being human
should have gained enough acumen
to know the outcome when they prod
against the firm-laid laws of God.

Thought for the Day: I know that surety lies within the bounds of God's precepts—and that is where I want to live.

JUNE 28

Scripture Reading: John 2:1-11

Verse for the Day: "Jesus and his disciples had also been invited to the wedding." (John 2:2)

The Ordinary Made Special

Not much is written about June,
except the heat it brings—too soon
for those who love the spring and hate to see it end.
But it's perfect for a honeymoon.

There's got to be a reason why
so many lovers often try
to set a wedding date within the month of June.
And could it be to satisfy

the need to find outside the maze
of months with other holidays
one in which the calendar is not already
filled with ceremonial craze?

The days or nights in June can be
that very special panoply,
when routine month becomes unique by sacred vow
that makes the he and she a "we."

Thought for the Day: It is within my power to make the ordinary special, for wherever and whenever I put God in the situation, the moment becomes extraordinary.

JUNE 29

Scripture Reading: Luke 6:32-38

Verse for the Day: "If you love those who love you, what credit is that to you? For even sinners love those who love them." (Luke 6:32)

What Credit?

If you love those who love you ...
that's an easy thing to do.
And Scripture says there's no reward—
no credit coming due.

Yet, if you're kind to those around
just for the gain and you are bound
by sordid motive, here again,
there's no credit to be found.

Hate-filled hearts still love their friends ...
can be charming when charm wins
approval or advantage
or a license for such sins.

But we must love our enemies!
And that is not achieved with ease.
It takes a lot of practice ... and
much time spent on the knees.

Thought for the Day: It's not easy to learn to love those we don't even like or who dislike us, but it's essential. I will do my best with God's help.

JUNE 30

Scripture Reading: I Thessalonians 5:12-21

Verse for the Day: "Pray without ceasing." (I Thessalonians 5:17)

Time to Pray

My spirit is so low today;
    I don't know why.
Instead of writing poetry,
    I want to cry.
My house needs a good cleaning, yet
    I don't want to.
My carport sale was such a bust;
    now I must do
away with all the junk that's left.
    I'm worried so
about my parents who still live
    alone although
they're not able; yet, won't agree
    to any change ...
to any in-house help or step
    to rearrange
things as they are. That's why I know
    I must commune
with God just now to get my soul
    and self in tune.

Thought for the Day: We are told to pray without ceasing; it's probably so that we would not have time to worry.

ENTERTAINING ANGELS

July

JULY 1

Scripture Reading: Hebrews 13:1-3

Verse for the Day: "Do not neglect to show hospitality to strangers, for by doing that some have entertained angels without knowing it." (Hebrews 13:2)

Entertaining Angels

When still a child she gathered home the strays;
she'd ask her mother if they couldn't keep
the dogs and cats—flea-covered, mangy grays—
the frightened turtle which would barely peep
from under its brown fortress of a shell.
She cradled in her little hands the bird
she spotted near the tree from which it fell.
And if some adult scolded with a word
of warning that such could be dangerous
she'd laugh and say, "Could be an angel, too."
She took her Sunday School quite serious.
She's older now and widowed but not through
providing help to any who appears.
She's entertained some angels through the years.

Thought for the Day: Today I will be more thoughtful of the strangers who cross my path, and if I am aware of a need I can meet, I will respond whether the needy appear angelic or not.

JULY 2

Scripture Reading: Ephesians 2:1-10

Verse for the Day: "For we are what he has made us, created in Christ Jesus for good works, which God prepared beforehand to be our way of life." (Ephesians 2:10)

The Recipe

Take the smallest, most inconsequential
morsel of truth you can think of;
add a dash of wit and wisdom; measure
carefully (in rhyme and rhythm) the love
of words and metaphor; add the rules
of good grammar to the ingredients
of experience and observation and intuition;
stir in a large portion of common sense;
mix well with creative artistry and let sit for
a while.

Then, with a generous ration of keen
insight, kneed the mixture and shape
pleasingly; top it all with the sheen
of a brilliant title. Serve warm without any
explanation—no matter when, why, or how.
And know you've made yourself a poem,
if your dish gets just one "Wow!"

Thought for the Day: Creative ability is a gift of God. Like God's own creativity, it comes in many forms, all of which, to be lasting, must be nurtured in good work.

JULY 3

Scripture Reading: Proverbs 25:11-28

Verse for the Day: "A word fitly spoken is like apples of gold in a setting of silver." (Proverbs 25:11)

Ah, But It Will

When I'd come home with a scratch on the car
even though it was new, he'd say,
"Well, we bought it to use, not to look at,"
and he'd laugh my worries away.

When I backed into the guest preacher's car
on the crowded church parking lot,
he said, "You didn't do it on purpose,
did you?" Then declared, "Of course not!"

But I really dreaded to call home when
I totaled the just paid-for car.
I knew he would surely explode this time,
saying this had gone too far.

He just rejoiced that no one was injured—
then with his typical good sense,
he hugged me close and said, "Five years from now
it won't make any difference."

Thought for the Day: The difference a kind word can make on a life is undeniable. When impatience and anger would threaten to overcome compassion, I pray for good humor and wise judgment.

JULY 4

Scripture Reading: Lamentations 5

Verse for the Day: "With a yoke on our necks we are driven; we are weary, we are given no rest." (Lamentations 5:5)

For Those Much Burdened

Oh my, it's July!
June ended too soon.
It's hot, and what
is more there are bugs galore.
And no rain again
but humidity! Pity
the one who works in the sun
or anywhere the air
is stifling! It's not trifling
to wish for a day with relief on the way—
for a breeze to ease
the strain and stress. Yes,
I *shall* remember
        those cold in December.

Thought for the Day: A thoughtful person is aware of all the conditions that make life hard for others. I shall try to be sensitive to the needs that natural phenomenon can create.

JULY 5

Scripture Reading: Psalm 95

Verse for the Day: "In his hands are the depths of the earth; the heights of the mountains are his also." (Psalm 95:4)

The Common Air

I breathe "the common air that bathes the globe;"
that air Walt Whitman breathed when penning those
and other words that came to be the strobe
of light for generations in the throes
of selfish, indulgent gentility.
The lawn I walk upon grows from the seeds
of grass that ancient peoples saved for me.
The thoughts I think that detail all my needs
are the same thoughts that brought the captured
      slaves
and bought and sold them—indeed, the same
      thoughts
the enslaved had, of freedom and of graves—
heights and depths of emotional onslaughts.

The same God met on peak of sunny height
meets us when we land in the depth of night.

Thought for the Day: I will remember that all people have the same longings, needs, and selfish inclinations. But we also have in common a God who understands and meets us where we are.

JULY 6

Scripture Reading: Isaiah 14:1-7

Verse for the Day: "The whole world is at rest and quiet; they break forth into singing." (Isaiah 14:7)

Of Song and Silence

A song of peace that every living thing
may learn—for this I pray, O Lord.
A song of praise ecstatic souls may sing,
a psalm of tribute to your word.

And when this voice gives way, let me be still
an instrument whose one intent
is to remain in awe of Divine Will,
which decrees that, in the silent

dignity of the being's inner space
there is a holy harmony—
a lyrical accord of time and place,
of nature, earth, and sky, and sea.

a melody that every living thing
may know. Lord, let me see
that the peace I seek—for which I sing—
is nowhere found if not in me.

Thought for the Day: Hymns and songs of praise have been a blessing to my life. But the music must reach my soul if I would be an instrument of God.

JULY 7

Scripture Reading: Mark 10:23-30

Verse for the Day: "For mortals it is impossible, but not for God; for God all things are possible." (Mark 10:27b)

All Things Are Possible

They said he would not walk again;
      they did not know
the strength of will which drove him on.

It did not matter how much pain
      or just how slow
the process—it was his alone.

He did not let himself despair;
      he set a goal,
and he would make it—come what may!

Some days were good, some bad, some fair.
      He would be whole;
that thought sustained him night and day.

For years his spirit fortified
      those close at hand;
his zeal became a sacred vow.

And then, quite suddenly, he died.
      But understand,
he did not fail—he's walking now!

Thought for the Day: When we do the very best we can, the results must be left in God's hands. For there, all things are possible.

JULY 8

Scripture Reading: I Corinthians 1:1-9

Verse for the Day: "... together with all those who in every place call on the name of our Lord Jesus Christ ..." (I Corinthians 1:2b)

Preoccupation

He never hears a word she says—
claims he's preoccupied;
then says she never told him, though,
so many times she tried.

A friend says she'll return her call—
can't take the time today
to tell her of the trip to France,
but wants to right away.
Yet, time goes by; no call returned.

Preoccupation ends
another friendship, for always
it takes two to be friends.

She knows she's not important—
has very little clout—
feels not worth being listened to
or hearing all about
a trip to Paris in the spring.

But still she knows she can confide
in One who hears—returns her calls—
is not preoccupied.

Thought for the Day: Human relationships, however close, cannot be counted on for personal fulfillment. I must stay close to God, who can.

JULY 9

Scripture Reading: Jeremiah 17:7-10

Verse for the Day: "Blessed are those who trust in the Lord, whose trust is the Lord; they shall be like a tree planted by water ..." (Jeremiah 17:8a)

By the Waters

I stood beside a lively stream,
a shimmering, tumbling, crystal dream
of pure water that mesmerized.

I sensed a cleansing capsulized
in completeness seldom felt.

There on the grassy bank I knelt
to thank the one whose spirit power
had soaked into me like a shower.

I leaned against the sturdy elm—
a tiny speck within God's realm—
stunned and amazed at what I knew
to be improbable, but true.

Who made the earth and all above
had just communed with me in love.

Thought for the Day: I want to be among those who love God's natural laws and realize they are meant for my benefit to be instruments by which my life is brought into harmony with God's will.

JULY 10

Scripture Reading: James 1:22-27

Verse for the Day: "Religion that is pure and undefiled before God, the Father, is this: to care for orphans and widows in their distress, and to keep oneself unstained by the world." (James 1:27)

To Be Blessed

An acquaintance of mine used to say,
when opening his mail every day,
"I hope it's not someone
asking me for my 'mon,'
'cause I ain't gonna give it away."

I told him one time what I thought
but I never was sure that he bought
into my theory
that each request should be
viewed as a blessing and sought.

For I think we're much blessed if we tend
to find ourselves on the "giving end,"
instead of the pleading
and forever needing.
Now that would be dreadful, my friend.

Thought for the Day: I will remember that to be on the giving end is to be blessed. I will be thankful for each opportunity and never begrudge the request.

JULY 11

Scripture Reading: Matthew 14:25-33

Verse for the Day: "And early in the morning he came walking toward them on the sea." (Matthew 14-25)

Walkin' on Water

When things were going right he'd say,
"Oh, yes, my darlin' daughter,
everything is as right as rain ...
and I'm walkin' on water."
I never knew quite what he meant
by "right as rain," but during
springtime showers I could share
his water walk alluring.
We'd drudge the slushy pasture lands
to check on calving cattle,
and, finding newborn in the herd,
he'd set about to battle
the elements to bring the cow
and calf home to the barn stall.
Then with them safely ensconced there
he'd proudly survey it all.
And say, with pat upon my head,
"Oh, yes, my darlin' daughter,
everything is as right as rain ...
and I'm walkin' on water."
He's gone now, but I still can hear
echoes of that quaint refrain
and almost see him beckon me
to go walkin' in the rain.

Thought for the Day: Good childhood memories are a source of happiness and strength. I want to help create good memories for children.

JULY 12

Scripture Reading: Proverbs 22:6-11

Verse for the Day: "Train children in the right way, and when they are old, they will not stray." (Proverbs 22:6)

Our Library

When we were small our mother read to my
brother and me two books we thought such fun;
A Child's Garden of Verses and *Treasure
Island* by Robert Louis Stevenson.

As soon as she would finish we'd begin
to beg that she would read again the best
parts; we'd chant ... "Yo, ho, ho, and a bottle
of rum. Sixteen men on a dead man's chest."

Or we would act out ... "I have a little
shadow ..." and one of us would always be
the shadow who goes in and out, whose use
the poet was never able to see.

Then, much to our delight, our mother would
agree to start the books again, and we
would lean against her chair and listen as
from night to night she read and made us see,

before bed, a world of adventure in
story suspenseful and pictures in rhyme.
We did not care that "Treasure ..." and "Garden ..."
were the only books we owned at the time.

Thought for the Day: It takes such a little of material things to broaden the world of a child. But it does take time.

JULY 13

Scripture Reading: Hebrews 13:5-8

Verse for the Day: "Keep your lives free from the love of money, and be content with what you have." (Hebrews 13: 5a)

Conversation

I looked up through the skylight
at the branches overhead;
a little star peeped through the leaves,
looked down at me, and said,
"How come you're so unhappy,
so discontent, distressed?
Could it be your grumbling self
has got you all depressed?"
I was at first offended;
"How dare you," I inquired,
"imply that I'm a grumbler?
I just can't get inspired.
I'm short of money every month
and under such a stress.
I must keep up appearances;
I've clients to impress."
"How many people in this world,"
it said, "would love to sleep
beneath a skylight with the stars
as company to keep?"
I thought about that ... then I vowed
to stop demanding, "Why?"
Instead, to count my blessings
and just enjoy the sky.

Thought for the Day: Instead of grumbling about things that are lacking in my life, I will focus on the things to enjoy, many of which don't cost a cent.

JULY 14

Scripture Reading: I Corinthians 3:18-23

Verse for the Day: "For the wisdom of this world is foolishness with God. For it is written, 'He catches the wise in their craftiness.'" (I Corinthians 3:19)

Worldly Wisdom

She stealthily plotted every move;
was smart beyond her learning.

Indulgence was more than weakness—
as was her ceaseless yearning

for more and more, a grasping fetish
that would, sooner or later,

destroy the very life she treasured,
which served but to inflate her

ego and turned out to be beyond
her controllability.

With all her "smart" she never achieved
discernment or stability.

Thought for the Day: There is a virtue, beyond learning, dependent on a higher power. It is the gift of insight that the wisdom of the world may not recognize.

JULY 15

Scripture Reading: Psalm 23

Verse for the Day: "... He leads me beside still waters; he restores my soul." (Psalm 23:2b-3a)

Beside Still Waters

There's a little place
within each of us
where the still waters lie;
where the self is at peace,
where, from that point,
we can regroup and try
to corral the impish
impulses to run or hide
or punish others
for our inadequacies,
impulses to ignore
the pleading of brothers
and sisters and neighbors.

There, beside the still water,
God waits ... love-clad.
This centering-in place—where
each of us meets the divine—
is, in reality, a launchpad.

Thought for the Day: I will spend time each day beside the still waters to find the inspiration and strength to do what I am led to know needs doing.

JULY 16

Scripture Reading: Isaiah 38:14-20

Verse for the Day: "The living, the living, they thank you, as I do for this day." (Isaiah 38:l0a)

Mixed Emotions

Life is a series of mistakes
or a roller coaster ride of "thrills and chills,"
growth opportunities.
"Take your choice," the teacher said.

When my broken heart aches
or I'm laid low with undefined ills,
or I'm forced to my knees ...
I'm tempted to choose life in bed.

But when I've just won the prize,
or I've found what I lost,
or I'm falling in love ...
I would choose to hug the world.

It's not "all" or "nothing"—not wise
to feel helplessly tossed—
for there is sunshine or moonglow above
the clouds from which lightning is hurled.

Thought for the Day: When I am caught up in the worries of the moment, I will try to remember that life is the sum of all experiences—and there, in the present and beyond, is God.

JULY 17

Scripture Reading: Proverbs 21:15-30

Verse for the Day: "Whoever wanders from the way of understanding will rest in the assembly of the dead. Whoever pursues righteousness and kindness will find life and honor." (Proverbs 21:16,21)

The Lady

> She must never have a positive thought;
> if so, she never lets it off of her tongue.
> I feel so blue like I've had the flu
> whenever she's around, and I have bought
> into her mood, and it has covered and clung
> to my being. Always seeing
> the negative and quick to point it out,
> she seems not to care that her comments dig,
> are often cruel. The golden rule
> is not what this lady is all about.
> And as for "tact," she doesn't give a fig!
>
> A friend of hers who often goes around
> in her company, is the opposite.
> This counterpart of greater art
> in graciousness and talent is a sound
> and civilizing leverage for right.
> But lesser known she's sometimes thrown
> for a loop by the lady who has found
> that intimidation, not right, makes might!

Thought for the Day: I pray for the judgment to use, as a role model, the person who leaves me feeling better not worse and for the ability to be such a role model.

JULY 18

Scripture Reading: I Timothy 4

Verse for the Day: "For this end we toil and struggle, because we have our hope set on the living God, who is the Savior of all people, especially of those who believe." (I Timothy 4:10)

As the World Turns

I like a story with a happy ending—
a real love story with some suspense blending
uncertain romance with heart-stopping thrill,
till the very last moment when, in the still
unresolved conflict, the hero emerges,
is identified, and thwarts the vile surges
of evil intent—to right all wrongs and win.
Then, all is revealed, and the world turns again.

Unfortunately, it's only in fiction
that endings like that resolve all the friction.
Life, for the most part, is a series about
the ups and downs in a polyglot of doubt.
We all make it through from beginning to end
by trusting in God as creator and friend.

Thought for the Day: There may not be a happy ending to this day for me or someone I love, but I will continue to trust in a loving God whose will for me and everyone else is peace.

JULY 19

Scripture Reading: John 16:25-33

Verse for the Day: "I have said this to you, so that in me you may have peace. In the world you face persecution. But take courage; I have conquered the world." (John 16:33)

Next Door

My husband has his mother's house now that she's
gone;
he keeps it up and rents it out, but it is on
a street that is quickly changing. In fact, it's next
to a new parking lot, and that's got us perplexed,
for we've been told that we're zoned "residential."
And this is not a matter inconsequential.
The house on the other side is a noisy place,
filled with people of every age, size, sex, and race.
And they love music—loud, blaring music that
makes
the neighborhood rattle and roll—music that shakes
the rafters and drives the tenants to break their lease.
We'd like to rent to a business not needing peace
and quiet, but we're "residential," the City states.
It cannot bend the rules for us but tolerates
a rip-roaring party house and a parking lot.
Makes us wonder what those others have that we've
not
But, we've been told that life was meant not to be
fair
but challenging—and by golly, it's getting there!

Thought for the Day: Things will not always work out as we would like them to, but a sense of humor and goodwill is invaluable in handling frustration.

JULY 20

Scripture Reading: II Corinthians 9:6-15

Verse for the Day: "The point is this: the one who sows sparingly will also reap sparingly, and the one who sows bountifully will also reap bountifully. Each of you must give as you have made up your mind, not reluctantly or under compulsion, for God loves a cheerful giver."
(II Corinthians 9:6-7)

Generosity

The reaping may not always be at hand;
it may be though we sow throughout this life,
we find the harvest frustrating, the land
fallow, and the unproductive fields rife
with rocks and weeds. There are some who never
know the joy of gathering a full crop.
There may be years when, however clever
we view our creative effort to stop
erosion, bugs, freeze, or drought, there is no
reward. And yet, we're promised bountiful
harvest if we sow bountifully. So,
when are we to expect this miracle?
      The miracle is what the generous,
      unceasing sowing of seeds does to us.

Thought for the Day: A cheerful giver has a reward that others may not see and on which no income tax has to be paid.

JULY 21

Scripture Reading: Galatians 5:16-26

Verse for the Day: "Let us not become conceited, competing against one another, envying one another." (Galatians 5:26)

His Friend

His friend was so successful;
from high school right on through
his professional career
things fell in place on cue.

Always the faithful sidekick;
Joe remained in the shade
of the famous smile, aware
the other had it made.

But he was always happy
to be a step behind;
his genuine delight was
in trying to be kind.

And then one day his friend fell,
and even fame and pelf
could not reclaim the lost soul
who had destroyed himself.

Joe remained throughout the trial
a true, devoted friend
putting his own life on hold
until the bitter end.

Thought for the Day: Friendship and envy are incompatible, and sometimes those we're tempted to envy are more in need of friendship than we know.

JULY 22

Scripture Reading: Ecclesiastes 2:14-26

Verse for the Day: "There is nothing better for mortals than to eat and drink, and find enjoyment in their toil. This also, I saw, is from the hand of God; for apart from him who can eat or who can have enjoyment?" (Ecclesiastes 2:24-25)

After Vacation

"Did you enjoy your vacation?"
friends asked when I returned.
I answered, "Yes, except the day
I got badly sunburned."

I did enjoy the mountains and
the lakes and cabins quaint.
I felt each day that I communed
with Nature's patron saint.

I picked wild flowers and berries
to make bouquets and pies;
at evening I would watch the sun
set where the treeline lies.

I'm glad there is vacation time,
to charge the battery ...
and then, revitalized, I'm glad
there's still a job for me.

Thought for the Day: How fortunate are those who have meaningful work to do and enjoy doing it. I know that with God's blessing all honorable labor can have meaning.

JULY 23

Scripture Reading: John 13:1-17

Verse for the Day: " So if I, your Lord and Teacher, have washed your feet, also you ought to wash one another's feet." (John 13:14)

Motive

When Jesus washed their feet,
despite the protest plea,
he said, "Unless I do,
you have no part of me."

So Peter and the rest
allowed the rendered rite;
for service, Christ proclaimed,
was precious in God's sight.

The status matters not;
or even attitude—
or if response is less
than humble gratitude.

We are not judged by the
response we get from those
we serve, but by our own
motive—and the Lord knows.

Thought for the Day: I will not base my charity on the response it engenders, but I will be grateful for opportunities to share and to serve.

JULY 24

Scripture Reading: James 4

Verse for the Day: "Humble yourselves before the Lord, and he will exalt you." (James 4:10)

Lessons

"If you can't say something nice
about someone or something,
say nothing." I spend a lot
of time now remembering
that which my mother taught me.
For, you see, she's no longer
able to remember. I
am now the one who's stronger—
who must do the teaching. It
is I who patiently
repeat the same instructions
time and again until she
knows what to do. And I say
nothing because there's nothing
good to say about that which
is steadily happening
to her, to us. But someday
soon, with the Alzheimer's lain
in the grave, she'll realize
her lessons were not in vain.

Thought for the Day: The Lord will help us to bear what might seem unbearable, and lessons in right-living, well-learned, will stand us in good stead.

JULY 25

Scripture Reading: II Corinthians 3

Verse for the Day: "Not that we are competent of ourselves to claim anything as coming from us; our competence is from God."
(II Corinthians 3:5)

Unaware

The birds that bathe in my backyard,
red and blue and yellow-crested,
have no idea what joy they are—
with what charm they've been invested.
They are guileless, without a hint
of artifice and false pretense.

The child who plays in father's shoes
acting grown-up in innocence
or gets in mother's make-up drawer
to smear lipstick on face and rugs
is not aware that such display
is what makes parents shutter bugs.

The bluebird or its counterpart—
the child who's innocent of heart—
are neither one aware their being
glorifies our bliss in seeing.

Thought for the Day: Innocence is a crown for created things. And what a pleasure to be around people who wear it ... who are blessings to others just by being.

JULY 26

Scripture Reading: Exodus 14

Verse for the Day: "... stretch out your hand over the sea and divide it, that the Israelites may go into the sea on dry ground." (Exodus 14:16b)

The "Soul of Me"

I've met the waters of race prejudice—
the waves of fear and insecurity—
the tide of despair that would scuttle this
fragile vessel known as the "Soul of Me."

I've stretched my hand out, seen waters recede,
and cautiously proceeded through the sea.
I've faced down currents that would sore impede
a faithful journey for the "Soul of Me."

I've seen the forces flanked in proud array
prepared to orchestrate catastrophe,
reached out my hand again in time to sway
the ocean and preserve the "Soul of Me."

I've found what one can do when pledged to be
a "soulmate" with the One who calms the sea.

Thought for the Day: Miracles still happen when the will of God and the willingness of individuals meet. I want to be a part of those miracles.

JULY 27

Scripture Reading: Proverbs 16:16-24

Verse for the Day: "How much better to get wisdom than gold. To get understanding is to be chosen rather than silver." (Proverbs 16:16)

The Streak

I keep the little things you made for me:
the "Mother" carved in wood hung on a string,
the pencil box, the tinfoil Christmas tree,
the lamp—pump-handled—an uncommon thing.

I treasure every funny word you said:
"wire duck" for "fire truck," "wind blowin' up me."
But clearer is the sight of your brown head
with streak of yellow hair when you were three.

Somewhat like a skunk's—right down the center—
that streak was prominent for many months.
Now, as gray flecks increasingly enter
your picture, my recollection still hunts

for just a hint of yellow in the curl
of brown-haired cherub who's your little girl.

Thought for the Day: Wisdom is in understanding that memories are best relived, not just in mind but in the heart's recall, and only those which find their way into the heart should be relived.

JULY 28

Scripture Reading: Genesis 9:1-17

Verse for the Day: "I have set my bow in the clouds, and it shall be a sign between me and the earth, for all future generations." (Genesis 9:13)

My Rainbow

There is a rainbow in my sky;
an arc of multi-colored hues.
It's always there to certify
that if I win or if I lose
God's promise covers even me.
And when the raging storm within
would beat upon my certainty,
I glimpse a rainbow through the din.
I rest upon that vivid vow
God made when setting out the sign
of many colors which is now
the special rainbow that is mine.

Thought for the Day: I know that God's promises are as personal as they are universal. I will continue to rely on a personal relationship with God.

JULY 29

Scripture Reading: Jeremiah 38:1-20

Verse for the Day: "... Just obey the voice of the Lord in what I say to you, and it shall go well with you, and your life will be spared." (Jeremiah 38:20b)

The Wonder

When Jeremiah prophesied
  he met with such resistance
he ended up down in a well
  at his enemy's insistence.
The king confronted with his guilt
  at letting Jeremiah
encounter such a fate as this
  began to wonder why a
prophet of the Lord would make such
  dreadful, dire predictions,
so he allowed God's spokesman to
  escape the well's restrictions.
Then, Jeremiah secretly
  pronounced the king's own fate.
Unless he would obey the Lord,
  he and his house would rate
misfortune and destruction and
  his kingdom would be done for.
And so it was; and so it is;
  then, now, and ever more.
The lessons of the Bible teach
  that what went on back yonder
is portent of what will transpire.
  When will we learn, I wonder!

Thought for the Day: Biblical history, like any other, is meant to teach. We learn, as a world, a nation, an individual, or the lesson will be repeated.

JULY 30

Scripture Reading: I Timothy 6:1-8

Verse for the Day: "Of course, there is great gain in godliness combined with contentment." (I Timothy 6:6)

To Be Content

We can search the world over and never find
the contentment we're seeking—the peace of mind.

> For if it's not found in the backyard at home
> it won't be located in Athens or Rome
> or Paris, Calcutta, Madrid, Singapore,
> or London or Cairo or a multitude more.

The search will be endless; serenity breached—
an illusion until we've looked inward and reached
the God who is ready to faithfully give
the peace and contentment in which we would live.

> We may search the world over only to find
> contentment is being in God's state of mind.

Thought for the Day: It's never too late to realize that peace and contentment and godliness are inevitably intertwined and not a matter of place or situation.

JULY 31

Scripture Reading: Hebrews 3:1-6

Verse for the Day: "(For every house is built by someone, but the builder of all things is God.)" (Hebrews 3:4)

The Builder

He or she who builds
is close to the divine.
One who constructs a house
is in a long, long line
of those who follow in
the hallowed tradition
of the carpenter whose
holy intuition
led him to become a
contractor for the Lord,
with commission to build
(without stone, brick, or board)
the Kingdom of God
in the hearts of all.

He or she who builds
has surely heard the call,
and, when surveying work
completed, must admit
the most admired result
comes with God's hand in it.

Thought for the Day: Those who build must surely be aware of whose footsteps they follow.

GRACE SUFFICIENT

August

AUGUST 1

Scripture Reading: Romans 11:1-16

Verse for the Day: "But if it is by grace, it is no longer on the basis of works, otherwise grace would no longer be grace." (Romans 11:6)

Grace Sufficient

"Ah, there, but for the grace of God."
How many times has that been said!
It seems to indicate that God's
grace has settled on one instead
of the other. Does grace not reach
to the outer edge and beyond?
To the bottom of the bottle ...
to the mind over which the wand
of fantasy has waved away
rational thought ... to the barred gate
and locked cell of the cold prison ...
to the bed in the wooden crate
under the bridge? If not for grace
which notes impartiality
and mercy for the "least of these,"
then I would not be free.
I've learned that God's grace covers all.
I don't know how; I don't know why.
But I do know it's best to say,
"There **by** the grace of God go I."

Thought for the Day: Humanity, all of it, is basically in the same boat, needing God's grace to stay afloat. To look in the waters of human need is to look in a mirror.

AUGUST 2

Scripture Reading: Isaiah 58:9-14

Verse for the Day: "... you shall be like a watered garden, like a spring of water, whose waters never fail." (Isaiah 58:11b)

The Children Must Have Water

City children must have water, too—
fresh, cool, pure water in which to swim,
where they can splash away their troubles—
feel its healing power over them.

Urban children must have gardens, too,
where they can watch the flowers grow—
tend the soil, plant the seed, water the growth.
observe the miracle. They must know

that God's at work on city streets as well
as in the countryside ...
that God's love crosses city limits
and spans concrete buildings high and wide.

Children of the streets must know that there's
a spring of "living water" which won't fail—
which flows liberatingly even
through weed-choaked garden to the narrow trail.

Thought for the Day: I must never become calloused to needs or to think that others who don't have the advantages I have are unworthy. One person's need is another's challenge.

AUGUST 3

Scripture Reading: II Corinthians 5:16-21

Verse for the Day: "So if anyone is in Christ, there is a new creation; everything old has passed away; see, everything has become new." (II Corinthians 5:17)

The Acorn

The acorn—cap and gown—
who knows what glory,
what moment of renown,
lies within that story?
Will the squirrel store
it under leafy bed?
Will bluejay bore
a hole in amber head?
Will a mighty oak
sprout at graduation?
Or will some careless bloak
heedless of its station
trample it under booted foot?
I've even seen its face
painted, false lashes put
on and big lips in place,
or with others glued,
then called an acorn-doll.
Its fate can be askewed
like ours—from painted moll
or shady character,
to giant of the wood
by environmental factor,
reflecting bad or good.

Thought for the Day: Circumstances may shape us in ways we deplore. It's up to me to accept God's promise to reshape my life as a new creation.

AUGUST 4

Scripture Reading: Luke 12:22-28

Verse for the Day: "Consider the lilies, how they grow, they neither toil nor spin; yet, I tell you, even Soloman in all his glory was not clothed like one of these." (Luke 12:27)

The Flower Child

At birth her parents named her Daffodil,
and though they called her Daffy she would be
a flower in life's garden and would fill
their home with golden sunshine—fleeting—free.

"Good morning, Buttercup," she always said,
as she passed smiling jonquils in the yard.
The answer was a lift of yellow head
and wave of green leaf-blade which stood at guard.

The jonquils knew that Daffy was their kind;
grace like hers is only found in flowers.
She bears a regal presence one would find
mainly in cascading floral bowers.

When other blooms have bowed to summer-kill,
the brighter blossoms lovely Daffodil.

Thought for the Day: I want to furnish for those about me a bouquet of happiness that does not wilt in heat nor wither in frost. Today I will begin to fashion that bouquet.

AUGUST 5

Scripture Reading: Romans 7:1-12

Verse for the Day: "... so that we are slaves not under the old written code, but in the new life of the Spirit." (Romans 7:6b)

On an Anniversary

Thirty-nine years ... I remember fifteen
and thinking I had been married forever.
But a lot has happened between
then and now. I would never
have thought we would make it.
The time went by so fast,
taxing nerve and will and wit.
Yet, now that it is passed,
our backs a bit bent,
our children grown,
we wonder where it went.
Just you and me ... alone ...
the way it was back when
we started out together.
Yet, let's not dwell on "then,"
instead, I think I'd rather
just let you know
that when today is through
I'm ready to go
thirty-nine more with you.

Thought for the Day: Time spent looking back or living in the past is time wasted. I want to make the most of today and stay optimistic about the future.

AUGUST 6

Scripture Reading: Habakkuk 3

Verse for the Day: "Though the fig tree does not blosson, and no fruit is on the vines ... yet I will rejoice in the Lord." (Habakkuk 3:17a, 18a)

Yet I Will Rejoice

When floods take fields of topsoil,
or our land is scorched with drought,
we're tempted to forsake our trust,
give way to fear and doubt.

When sunshine is for others
while dark clouds hang overhead,
we often feel ourselves forsaken,
facing the future with dread.

We're lured to deep forebodings
by human inclinations;
we talk ourselves into a panic
by profane incantations.

Let us rejoice, be thankful
the Lord still rules over wrong...
that even when things are looking bad,
God gives the righteous a song.

Thought for the Day: Today I will concentrate, not on the things that go wrong, but on the promise of God's ever-abiding presence.

AUGUST 7

Scripture Reading: Hosea 14:1-7

Verse for the Day: "They shall again live beneath my shadow, they shall flourish like a garden." (Hosea 14:7)

God's Shadow

Like a giant oak or redwood
sheltering the forest floor,
the shadow of the Almighty
makes an awning for my door.

When the heat of day would stifle,
draining will and strength away.
under the divine umbrella
of God's shadow I would stay.

When the blazing sun would blister,
render heat-stroke, even death,
I would sit in cooling comfort
in celestial shadow's breath.

And I'll flourish like a garden;
for if I will do my part
to remain beneath God's shadow,
I'll grow up into God's heart.

Thought for the Day: We become like that with which we associate and identify. If I would grow spiritually, I must stay close to the divine Spirit.

AUGUST 8

Scripture Reading: II Samuel 18

Verse for the Day: "The king was deeply moved, and went up to the chamber over the gate, and wept, and, as he went, he said, 'O my son Absalom, my son, my son! (II Samuel 18:33)

A Father's Love

When Absalom rebelled against his father,
King David never ceased to love his son,
and when the battle of the mighty warriors
was over, and the victory was won ...

King David's heart was broken for he found
his son was slain by servants of the king,
who, though he was the ruler, had not the power
sufficient to prevent this dreadful thing.

"Oh, Absalom, Absalom, my son, my son!"
he cried, and vowed that he would willingly
have died instead of Absalom, for that's
the way a loving father tends to be.

Thought for the Day: God's love is, above all, that of a good parent, unconditional. It is incumbent upon each of us to accept divine counsel, forego rebellion, and be a good son or daughter.

AUGUST 9

Scripture Reading: II Thessalonians 3:6-17

Verse for the Day: "Brothers and sisters, do not be weary in doing what is right." (II Thessalonians 3:13)

Responsibility

Others may not do their share;
but what is that to me?
I'm responsibly aware
of what's required. I see
the needs that I can attend:
the hungry I can feed,
the broken hearts I can mend,
the crime which grows from seed
of neglect that I can shine
a spotlight on. How much
more gets done if I don't whine
about others as such
slackards and offer excuse
for my sloth by pointing
to them. I must forego that ruse
in favor of working.

Thought for the Day: I'm not responsible for what others fail to do or how far short they fall of the mark. But I am responsible for me.

AUGUST 10

Scripture Reading: John 6:35-51

Verse for the Day: "No one can come to me unless drawn by the Father who sent me." (John 6:44a)

Unless Drawn

"No one can come unless drawn;"
yet only those drawn are
those inclined in the direction
of the holy. No bar
exists that artifically
prohibits humanity
from approaching the divine.
"Whosoever will," we
are told in other spaces.
It's up to you and me
as to whether we are drawn.
God stands at the door and knocks;
would wish all who hear respond,
but will not breach the locks
or coerce hospitality.
Unless we keep our minds
and hearts out in the open...
unless the Lord's pull finds
us receptive—ready and willing
to be drawn—we will stay
in unlighted rooms behind locked doors
well back from the highway.

Thought for the Day: It's up to me to keep myself in the position to be drawn. When God calls I can answer only if I am listening.

AUGUST 11

Scripture Reading: II Corinthians 2:12-17

Verse for the Day: "But thanks be to God, who in Christ always leads us in triumphal procession, and through us spreads in every place the fragrance that come from knowing him." (II Corinthians 2:14)

All Hail

The knowledge of God is sweet,
like fresh-felled grass
or prairie sunset or fleet-
footed fawns which pass
before quick-focused eyes
or early autumn breeze
spreading divine knowledge—in guise
of fragrant fervencies—
that no matter the outcome,
the Lord will prevail.

And those who are not numb
to God's will shall hail
Godly counsel and caring
till victory is won.

Lord, lead me in sharing
the triumph of your son.

Thought for the Day: If, as I believe, God is love, then staying close to that love is to my advantage, and sharing the knowledge of God's identity is simply kindness to others.

AUGUST 12

Scripture Reading: Ruth 2:8-23

Verse for the Day: "May the Lord reward you for your deeds, and may you have a full reward from the Lord, the God of Israel, under whose wings you have come for refuge." (Ruth 2:12)

Her Presence

She offered comfort in the only way she knew.
she whispered as she hugged me, "I love you."

"I'm sorry," others say and hold my hand.
And that is fine; it lets me know they understand.

But hers, a special touch; it's always there ...
not only in foul weather, but in fair.

When times are good she is the one
to share a laugh—a moment in the sun.

But, oh, how necessary is her presence when
a-hurting is the state my heart is in.

Thought for the Day: I want to be the kind of friend whose presence is a joy in good times and a comfort in bad. Lord, make me sensitive to the needs of others.

AUGUST 13

Scripture Reading: Nehemiah 2:11-20

Verse for the Day: "Then they said, 'Let us start building!' So they committed themselves to the common good." (Nehemiah 2:18b)

Commitment

> Commitment builds a temple;
> commitment builds a life;
> commitment is what makes things work
> for a husband and a wife.
>
> Committed doesn't mean possessed;
> the connotation is
> unselfishness—the common good—
> a mutual state of bliss.
>
> It's not the one who does most;
> it's not the one who knows;
> but success comes to the one whose
> commitment to it grows.
>
> As long as there are people
> whose goal—"thy will be done"—
> is something they're committed to,
> God's kingdom will still come.

Thought for the Day: I know that the kingdom of God is within, and I want it to be within me. I know, too, that commitment is the key.

AUGUST 14

Scripture Reading: I Peter 1:3-16

Verse for the Day: "Therefore prepare your minds for action; discipline yourselves; set all your hope on the grace that Jesus Christ will bring you when he is revealed." (I Peter 1:13)

Glad Tidings

"Prepare your minds for action.
discipline yourselves; set all
your hope on the grace that Christ
brings." Some people think a pall
of somber ambiance must
accompany a devout
mind and spirit, but not so.
Rather, what it's all about
is action, discipline, grace,
and hope; such forward-looking
attitudes are put in place
by devotion to the cause
of Christ. Sometimes it seems there's
a conspiracy to squelch
the Spirit through conscious airs
of superiority
or long-faced, dire predictions.
But, Christianity is for
those with glad predilections.

Thought for the Day: If I am faithful to the good news, then my countenance and my attitude will reveal a good spirit within—hopeful, disciplined, and active.

AUGUST 15

Scripture Reading: Genesis 32:1-12

Verse for the Day: "I am not worthy of the least of all the steadfast love and all the faithfulness that you have shown to your servant ..."
(Genesis 32:10b)

The Ordinary

Little children the world over
play their games of hide-and-seek,
look for treasures in the rubble,
long to splash in cool, clear creek.

Children find in ordinary
things the stuff of life and joy;
look to their imaginations,
making rocks and boxes toys.

Why is it that complications
come increasingly with age?
Why can't we be as the children,
capable at every stage

of recognizing worth as truly
that which comes from humble heart;
lasting value in the mundane;
simple living as an art?

Thought for the Day: Probably today will find me doing very ordinary things. My attitude will make all the difference. Lord, let me be worthy of the day.

AUGUST 16

Scripture Reading: Psalm 36

Verse for the Day: "Your steadfast love, O Lord, extends to the heavens, your faithfulness to the clouds. Your righteousness is like mighty mountains, your judgments are like the great deep; you save humans and animals alike." (Psalm 36:5-6)

Holy Ground

God's love is painted on this earth's landscape.
Blue vaulting heavens hold the gaze in awe
when charmed visitors view the mountain's drape
of glist'ning snow in sunlight, as the thaw
brings streams of crystal rivers down the slope.
We can't begin imagining how deep
the oceans really are or how to cope
with all of nature's power; how to keep
the special balance of the atmosphere.
In the presence of the phenomenal
beauty surrounding tenants of this sphere,
God's greatest gift is still the powerful
assurance that we're loved, that God is found
wherever earth is viewed as "holy ground."

Thought for the Day: I will remember that God's love for creation is what keeps the earth spinning, at least for today, and that the "love" which is God's nature is meant for all.

AUGUST 17

Scripture Reading: Romans 8:1-17

Verse for the Day: "For all who are led by the Spirit of God are children of God." (Romans 8:14)

In Him

The Spirit lives in him—
that's obvious to those
who know. He always tries
to settle strife and close
the generation gap
between his age and youth.
His handshake is his vow;
his given word, the truth.
If only there were more
of his kind on this earth—
more who found real strength
in love and joy. No dearth
of goodness seen in him—
he's kindness to the core.
He's found his own salvation
as God's ambassador.

Thought for the Day: It's true that the only gospel some people will hear is, not what I say, but what I do. If what I do is the "good news," it will be effective.

AUGUST 18

Scripture Reading: Proverbs 11:25-32

Verse for the Day: "The fruit of the righteous is a tree of life ..." (Proverbs 11:30a)

Tree-Like

A bravely patient tree
leaning leafless in the wind
holding on to promises
that winter, too, will end,
reminds me of the one
who clings to life's poetry
while tempted to believe
that now is eternity.
     Though buffeted by storm,
the tree waits to welcome spring,
assured of new leaf buds,
nesting birds returned to sing,
and children playing underneath
its green canopy.
Nothing in the winter freeze
portends what is to be.
     So the one oppressed, despondent,
challenged more than most,
who manages to hold to faith
that heaven's high host
will bring to pass another spring,
yet another day,
is the one who then can show
the less tree-like the way.

Thought for the Day: When everything is going well, it's easy to be faithful. I am thankful for the example of those who hold on to faith when things look bad.

AUGUST 19

Scripture Reading: Romans 13:11-14

Verse for the Day: "Besides this, you know what time it is, how it is now the moment for you to wake from sleep." (Romans 13:11a)

Now Is the Season

Each season is a fantasy
a canvass where it seems that there's
an artist waving wand about.
      God, let us know that come the fall,
      this summer set the stage for all.
But let's not rush to leafless tree
ignoring summer's breathless airs.
Let's stay outdoors, defy heat's clout.

It soon is gone; there is no doubt.
Anticipation often dares
us not admire the times we see.
      God, let us stop, enjoy the bliss
      of season's beauty, even this ...
And then, through fall and winter's shout,
we'll cast our lot on daily prayers
and trust the Lord that spring will be.

Thought for the Day: Let me not rush through life living in anticipation of the next day, the next season, the next year without fully appreciating the present.

AUGUST 20

Scripture Reading: Lamentations 3: 21-26

Verse for the Day: "The steadfast love of the Lord never ceases, his mercies never come to an end. They are new every morning; great is your faithfulness." (Lamentations 3:22-23)

Autumn

Today I felt the first faint hint of fall;
the breeze kicked up by morning smelled of change ...
a crisp response to atmospheric call
that renders seasons in and out of range.

I'll marshall all the forces of my will
to wait out temperatures one hundred plus,
for now I know that just over the hill
the autumn waits to bring relief to us.

I had another hint as day wore on:
a south-bound flock of birds flew overhead.
My mother used to say when birds were gone,
her summer-loving heart filled up with dread.

But I love fall; to me it always seems
the fountain from which springs the new year's dreams.

Thought for the Day: Each season is its own best ambassador, with beauty and fulfillment for those who enjoy life in this wonder-filled world God has created.

AUGUST 21

Scripture Reading: Joel 2:23-32

Verse for the Day: "I will pour out my spirit on all flesh; your sons and your daughters shall prophesy; your old men shall dream dreams, and your young men shall see visions." (Joel 2:28)

Do Not Disturb!

"On all who will receive it,
God's spirit is poured out!"
That's what he claimed as
he wandered all about
the town, muttering to himself
Some thought he'd be
better off locked up
in a mental ward where he
would not disturb. But then,
I don't know of anyone
he actually ever disturbed.
He never had a gun
or any weapon at all.
He never threatened or
postured so as to call
attention to himself roaming around
muttering about God's spirit.
Maybe those who were bothered
just didn't want to hear it!

Thought for the Day: Often I call disturbing something that I just don't want to think about. Maybe we're meant to be disturbed occasionally.

AUGUST 22

Scripture Reading: Luke 12:42-49

Verse for the Day: "I came to bring fire to the earth, and how I wish it were already kindled." (Luke 12:29)

Fire on the Earth

> Baptismal fire? Not water?
> Inconceiveable!
> God at the core of self ...
> the "Word" viable
> and internalized ...
> the flame which spread
> throughout the land.
> Even raised the dead;
> gave sight to blind; made
> deaf ear hear; exposed
> righteous charade.
> The mute led in song
> when tongs of fire touched tongue.
> No powers could put out
> the baptismal fire wrung
> from Holy Ghost. Natural;
> kindled through Christ by God,
> unquenchable!

Thought for the Day: The fire that God ignites in the hearts of those who are touched by the holy, should be incendiary. Do those who get close to me sense the heat?

AUGUST 23

Scripture Reading: Hebrews 13:7-21

Verse for the Day: "Jesus Christ is the same yesterday and today and forever." (Hebrews 13:6)

Moving Day

Morning breaks on moving day;
change is hard whichever way
it goes. But leaving known,
even for city I'd grown
up in, is difficult.
A lot of inner tumult
right now. I've got good friends here
and "back there" seems like clear
across a lifetime. In fact,
it is. I've truly wracked
my brain in an effort to
remember those I once knew
who still live there. I now must
rely more on the trust
I have in God. So here
I go, Lord, please stay near.

Thought for the Day: Change is always unsettling, and I must remember to be patient, not only with the inevitable changes in my life but in holding fast the faith that God does not change.

AUGUST 24

Scripture Reading: Mark 8:1-10

Verse for the Day: "They ate and were filled; and they took up the broken pieces left over, seven baskets full. Now there were about 4000 people ..." (Mark 8:8-9a)

The Knowing Zone

You have seen the feeding
of the multitude
and felt not so alone.
You are near to tasting
more than food;
you're getting closer to the zone.

> You have seen the crowd's
> hunger satisfied;
> you've been witness to the sign.
> You have sensed that there's
> another side;
> you're closer to the line.

> > To reach beyond the loaves
> > and fishes
> > to where the bread of life is known
> > is to move beyond the realm
> > of wishes
> > into the "knowing zone."

Thought for the Day: I know that there is much more to life than the material, and I resolve to spend time each day looking in the direction of spiritual accomplishment.

AUGUST 25

Scripture Reading: I Thessalonians 5:9-13

Verse for the Day: "Esteem them very highly in love because of their work."
(I Thessalonians 5:13a)

Those Who Know

There are those whose nature is
to serve and to give of themselves.
Then there are those who remain
packaged and stashed on their own shelves
in small, self-contained bundles.
It isn't hard to spot the one
who's willing to get involved.
You'll find her where good things get done.

You'll see him where the spirit
of willingness is manifest
in accomplishment, like road
adoption, meals-on-wheels, the best
health-care, good schools, well-funded
libraries. These people know that
to win this game of living
each one must take a turn at bat.

Thought for the Day: Thank heaven for those willing souls who share their lives with others in helpful deeds. I will use them as my role models.

AUGUST 26

Scripture Reading: Psalm 101

Verse for the Day: "I will walk with integrity of heart within my house; I will not set before my eyes anything that is base." (Psalm 101:2b-3a)

The View

He vowed to build for her a great house
with everything in it that pleasured
and with windows on the world she loved:
the mountains out beyond the treasured
city which was home to her since birth;
the lake on the other side of town;
a bird sanctuary at the back;
and, from the front, a lovely walk down
to the little church on the corner.
But, when dreams proved bigger than his will,
resolve failed; he left without goodbye.
And now she waits, for loving him still,
she can't imagine life without him.
She'd tell him if she could—mean it, too—
that she would be content in one room
with nothing but his sweet face to view.

Thought for the Day: When dreams collide with reality, it takes a strong faith in God to sustain us. Devotion, patience, and integrity of heart are the keys to survival.

AUGUST 27

Scripture Reading: II Corinthians 4:13-18

Verse for the Day: "... because we look not at what can be seen, but what cannot be seen; for what can be seen is temporary, but what cannot be seen is eternal." (II Corinthians 4:18)

When You're Batting Zero

Her name was given as a reference
by someone who wanted to rent from me
and needed the apartment quickly; hence,
my call at 8:00 a.m. was placed to see
if I could talk to her before she left
for work—I had been told she worked—and so
I was stunned senseless, totally bereft
of words at her verbal attack, although
I had spoken politely, explaining
the reason for my call. She used words which
bear forgetting; but, soundly complaining,
in phrases that would leave a prime-time glitch
when censors got through, she told me she could
not care less what I wanted at that (blank)
ungodly hour. The idea that I would
interrupt her sleep! Mentally, I shrank,
stammered, "Thank you," and hung up. And, of course,
"Sorry!" would have been more appropriate.
But at that moment I had no resource
mentally, no rational thought or wit.
The moral to this story is ... always
get a "reference" for the reference
you request, prepare for life to amaze
you, and know that sometimes nothing makes sense.

Thought for the Day: Some days getting up can be a challenge, and having to face other's problems can be provoking. A sense of humor always helps.

AUGUST 28

Scripture Reading: Isaiah 8:11-9:2

Verse for the Day: "The people who walked in darkness have seen a great light." (Isaiah 9:2a)

God's Deliverance

From the beginning
faith in the right
was more than a vision.
"Let there be light"
was God's declaration
in praise of truth.
Dreams of the elderly,
plans of the youth,
all come together in
that brilliant glow
which shatters the darkness—
lets wisdom flow.

God's light reaches farther
than words can tell,
and light is deliverance
from sin's dark spell.
The one who now walks on
an unlighted path
has chosen the shadows—
the way of wrath.

Thought for the Day: I know that sin is the deliberate turning away from God. I can just as well deliberately choose to walk in the light of God's will.

AUGUST 29

Scripture Reading: Psalm 37:23-29

Verse for the Day: "... though we stumble, we shall not fall headlong, for the Lord holds us by the hand." (Psalm 37:24)

All Things Well

They said of Jesus,
"He does all things well."
We are called upon
to follow; to dwell
in perfection, where
resisting evil,
doing no harm, and
being merciful,
(while ever staying
close in devotion
to God) is the way.
We plumb the ocean
depths of God's patience,
and are forgiven
time and time again.
Yet, each time, driven
to note the distance
from heaven to hell,
we resolve again
to do all things well.

Thought for the Day: I know that my own will is not strong enough to do always what is right. Only in close companionship with God can I live up to my good intentions.

AUGUST 30

Scripture Reading: I Peter 1:22-25

Verse for the Day: "... love one another deeply from the heart." (1 Peter 1:22b)

August

In the heat of August
humid and singed,
sultry, dust-streaked
and dank. Hinged
between summer
and autumn—rare jewel—
remembering the late summer's
golden rule,
I'll stay in good humor
as temperatures blast—
for "friends true in August
are destined to last!"

Thought for the Day: I must remember that good humor and gratitude are the keys to surviving trying conditions and challenging situations.

AUGUST 31

Scripture Reading: II Peter 3:8-13

Verse for the Day: "But do not ignore this one fact, beloved, that with the Lord one day is like a thousand years and a thousand years are like one day." (II Peter 3:8)

The Gift

This is the day to use well.
"Now is the hour," goes the tune.
Handle with care—both the hour and the day
are over all too soon.

In the sight of the Lord a year
is just an hour when done.
A decade long is but a rising
and setting of the sun.

A century, to God, can pass
in the blinking of an eye.
Don't let the chance to live this moment
go and pass you by.

Don't let the hour slip away
and wonder where it went.
Today is a gift from God; that's why
we call it the present.

Thought for the Day: To God, time is not the limiting dimension it is to us, but it's all we have, and I will renew efforts to make good use of my time.

TIME AND CHANCE

September

SEPTEMBER 1

Scripture Reading: Ecclesiastes 9:11-18

Verse for the Day: "Again I saw that under the sun the race is not to the swift, nor the battle to the strong, nor bread to the wise, nor riches to the intelligent, nor favor to the skillful, but time and chance happen to all." (Ecclesiastes 9:11)

Burning Bridges

The days slip by so quickly that it seems
sometimes the past is nothing more than dreams,
and truth is, time and time again I've found
that burning bridges seldom make a sound.
Five years from now what difference will it make?
Who cares if probing little fingers break
that antique vase that came from Great Aunt May,
the one she gave us on our wedding day?
Why grieve if one half of the Bible stand
is lost or if that winter-white headband
I wore the evening you proposed to me
is torn to shreds like lacy filigree.
Or even if the dress I married in
winds up in some yard sale or Goodwill bin
when left behind as we moved out of state.
Things aren't the arbiters of worth. Just wait!
When years have gone and looking back from age,
with curtains closed on yet another stage ...
the truth is, if you're honest, you'll have found
that burning bridges seldom make a sound.

Thought for the Day: Bridges, however reliable, are just things, and our security should not be tied to them but to the reliability of God. Time and chance happen to all of us.

SEPTEMBER 2

Scripture Reading: Psalm 121

Verse for the Day: "I lift up my eyes to the hills—from where will my help come? My help comes from the Lord who made heaven and earth." (Psalm 121:1-2)

Lord, You Gave Me a Mountain

My grandma always sang about a mountain—
"Oh, Lord," she said, "you gave me one this time."
I never saw that mountain that you gave her;
I never even saw her try to climb
that little hill beyond the barn out yonder,
but I suppose she did when she was young.
I only know that when I went to see her,
while we did dishes that one song was sung
until I felt that mountain was the only
thing worth getting Grandma ever got.
And yet, I know my grandpa one time bought her
a registered Dalmatian she called Spot.

I now know mountains are divinely given
and that the climbing over them instills
a fortitude of spirit for the migrant—
so I, too, lift my eyes up to the hills.
My help, just like the help which Grandma needed,
comes from the Lord, and daily I will lift
my mountain and whoever climbs it with me
to God, Almighty, giver of the gift.

Thought for the Day: Sometimes the way children see things is more akin to reality than the way adults see them. But all of us need God's uplifting that guides us over the mountains we have to climb.

SEPTEMBER 3

Scripture Reading: Matthew 5:38-48

Verse for the Day: "Be perfect, therefore, as your heavenly father is perfect." (Matthew 5:48)

Only Human

"I'm only human," she would say,
excusing acts or words that hurt
someone ... but how she dearly loved
to step on toes or dish the dirt.

She gossiped even if it meant
constructing stories from thin air,
and often just her presence cast
a pall upon the whole affair.

But, to be human should uplift,
not shift the soul toward base and mean;
that "human" is the lowest known
denominator is obscene.

To treat another as if we
as "human" forfeited control
is to ignore the Lord's mandate—
perfection is the human goal.

Thought for the Day: After the example of Christ, and since there have been saints whose lives are exemplary, we know that "much better" on the road to "perfection" is reachable.

SEPTEMBER 4

Scripture Reading: Philippians 1:3-11

Verse for the Day: "And this is my prayer, that your love may overflow more and more with knowledge and full insight to help you to determine what is best ..." (Philippians 1:9-10a)

For a Friend

You know, O Lord, the testing that he faces;
you know the weakness that besets his soul;
you know he's stumbled through so many races
and how he always undershoots the goal.

You are aware of stresses and of tensions
that keep him stretched like a high, tight wire;
you know all of his secret apprehensions
and how his mundane life teems with desire.

You know all this and more, Lord, even so ...
you love him, and he needs so much to know!

Thought for the Day: We should never fail to pray for our family and friends as specifically as we can, realizing all along that God already knows, but keeping the needs over which we pray precise in our minds.

SEPTEMBER 5

Scripture Reading: Luke 7: 11-17

Verse for the Day: When the Lord saw her, he had compassion for her and said to her, "Do not weep." (Luke 7:13)

The Revelation

The widow mourned her son;
Christ knew her pain.
He touched the funeral bier;
the young man lived again.

To bring to life the dead
is not within our power ...
but we can reach the one who did
at any hour.

The mystery hidden well
for centuries past
which was revealed in Jesus Christ
was meant to last.

That revelation lives
embodied in the soul
of each whom the touch of Christ
has raised, restored, made whole.

Thought for the Day: God can be so close that reaching the divine is a matter of centering, through prayer and meditation, on the revelation that is already within us.

SEPTEMBER 6

Scripture Reading: Matthew 23:1-12

Verse for the Day: "The greatest among you will be your servant." (Matthew 23:11)

Who Would Be Great

Who would be great must serve—
must wash the road-sore feet
of those he travels with
or any he should meet.

Where need presents itself—
or anguish lurks about—
where hope has all but died,
smothered in dusty doubt,
there, one who would be great
must kneel with basin filled
and let the healing balm
of sweat and tears be spilled.

The one whose title talks
proud, empty word—not deed—
will be beneath the one
whose heart and hand both bleed.

About who will be first,
no argument holds weight;
the one who stoops to serve
is he who would be great.

Thought for the Day: There's nothing new about the concept of discipleship as service—what's radical about it is that it involves me, and I must take it seriously.

SEPTEMBER 7

Scripture Reading: Matthew 10:1-15

Verse for the Day: "You received without payment; give without payment." (Matthew 10:8b)

Without Payment

Next month, dear Mother, you'll be eighty-five,
and while your mind is gone,
(this poem won't mean a thing),
you're down to skin and bone,
have no more songs to sing ...
you're presence keeps my daddy yet alive.

He watches over you as though a child;
he cooks your every meal
and washes clothes each week;
feels every pain you feel
and listens as you speak,
though sometimes repetition drives him wild.

No payment would be adequate to keep
his loyalty in tact.
He's stressed beyond belief,
and yet, it is a fact,
that he will die of grief
when someday you will not wake up from sleep.

Thought for the Day: To give without thought of payment or reward is the true measure of love. And everywhere we look—if we look—we can find examples of self-sacrificing love.

SEPTEMBER 8

Scripture Reading: Daniel 2:20-23

Verse for the Day: "Blessed be the name of God from age to age, for wisdom and power are his. He changes time and seasons ..." (Daniel 2:20b-21a)

Autumn's Shawl

I see God in the crisp, cool autumn dawn;
in brilliant, bronze chrysanthemum.
I see divinity in turning leaves;
in sweet and juicy purple plum.

When golds and reds embellish apple trees
like Christmas lights on Christmas eve,
there's got to be a God above it all—
a force for good. I must believe!

I see God in the woods, leaf-carpeted,
where darting squirrels play hide-and-seek,
that game we mortals very often play
to circumvent divine mystique.

Yet, God still demonstrates such depth of care
in vivid shades of autumn's shawl,
that holiness must be identified
with dazzling miracle of fall.

Thought for the Day: God's hand is behind the beauty of this earth; whatever the season, there is evidence in the natural grandeur that this is God's world.

SEPTEMBER 9

Scripture Reading: Isaiah 50:4-9a

Verse for the Day: "Morning by morning he wakens—wakens my ear to listen as those who are taught. The Lord God has opened my ear ..." (Isaiah 50:4b-5a)

God's Whisper

Morning by morning,
God's whisper I hear.
Day after day to my mind,
to my ear
comes the voice of the Lord
penetratingly clear.

Lo, I am with you
as a fountain of power,
your guide and provider
through every hour.
Then I take my position
under God's promised bower.

God's seeking an entry
to each inner being—
to the mind, to the heart,
to the soul, to the seeing.
God's whisper each morning—
equipping and freeing!

Thought for the Day: I will be silent each morning and listen for the penetrating voice of God. I will wait for the "word" for the day.

SEPTEMBER 10

Scripture Reading: Psalm 31:9-16

Verse for the Day: "For I hear the whispering of many—terror all around!—
... But I trust in you, O Lord; I say, 'You are my God.'" (Psalm31:13a,14)

A Lament

> I live in an uncertain world,
> and insecurity
> besets my life and steals my joy;
> from unknown threats I flee.
> But Lord, I still believe in you
> and in your love for me
> and that your will for each life is
> that it be whole and free.
> The headlines in the morning news
> are cause for real alarm;
> the fact is, innocence alone
> will not protect from harm.
> It's bad out there, and yet I know
> you've watched the path I've trod;
> the past has shown that even through
> disaster, you are God.
> And while I often move with sense
> of doom most imminent—
> a doubting Thomas at his worst,
> with catastrophic bent,
> I know, Lord, that in crises past
> you've always seen me through.
> Whatever else I fail to do,
> I still believe in you.

Thought for the Day: A lament is a form of prayer that speaks very honestly of all our fears and doubts, but then reaffirms our awareness of God's presence and blessings.

SEPTEMBER 11

Scripture Reading: Habakkuk 2:1-4

Verse for the Day: "I will stand at my watchpost, and station myself on the rampart; I will keep watch to see what he will say to me ..." (Habakkuk 2:1a)

At the Watchpost

Right will win out in the end ...
God will speak up when it's time.
Though all of life may be uphill,
God is leading in the climb.

Light will break forth like the dawn ...
wrong will not rule through the day.
There will come in God's own time
evil's end through righteous sway.

Like the prophet let us stand,
watch and listen for God's voice;
hold to vision when distressed,
thankful that we've got a choice.

That we may in measured means
help to make the crooked straight,
ever faithful through the night,
meant to work and watch and wait.

Thought for the Day: There is evidence that God's judgment does finally silence the oppressor. As we work for justice, we need to watch and listen for the signs of God's leading.

SEPTEMBER 12

Scripture Reading: Genesis 32:24-32

Verse for the Day: "For I have seen God face to face, and yet my life is preserved." (Genesis 32:30b)

The Inmost Need

She felt her trust had been betrayed;
a friend had broken confidence.
Her inner feelings were arrayed
in face stone-like and eyes intense.

The breach, she thought, could never be
forgiven or forgotten, yet
the only hope that she could see
to salvage friendship was to let

the past be gone, accept the fact
that her best friend was human, too,
and try to keep goodwill in tact
by doing what she could not do.

Her friend came to apologize,
to beg forgiveness for the deed;
she seemed, at least, to recognize
that pardon was the inmost need.

The pardoned and the pardoner
both find forgiveness requisite,
lest each become the forfeiter
of grace—redemptive, infinite.

Thought for the Day: When we look into the face of God in Christ, we see forgiveness. Therefore, when others look at us, who would be Christ-like, they must see forgiveness.

SEPTEMBER 13

Scripture Reading: "She will bear a son, and you are to name him Jesus, for he will save his people from their sins." (Matthew 18:21)

Jesus, the Name

What's in a name?
Is it a game
parents play—
choosing for one
who has no say?
For a tiny son
or girl baby—
maybe
something sweet,
or neat,
or concocted as cute
which doesn't suit
at all,
but does enthrall
the imagination.

When Jesus was named
as the angel proclaimed
by coronation,
there was meaning to it—
a perfect fit.
For the name he gave
was "God will save."

Thought for the Day: It has been said that names shape individuals as much as individuals shape names. Even nicknames should not be conferred carelessly.

SEPTEMBER 14

Scripture Reading: Acts 14:12-18

Verse for the Day: "... he has not left himself without a witness in doing good—giving you rains from heaven and fruitful seasons, and filling you with food and your hearts with joy. (Acts 14:17)

Witness

The depth of God's love
is uncomprehendable.
We often ignore,
though they are dependable,
the portents of grace—
the plentiful signs
that love is at work:
in teachers who care,
in healers who sacrifice,
in neighbors aware,
in minds of great intellect,
in unselfish sweat,
in deeds of benevolence,
in needs daily met.

Swept up in the ruthless
routine of the headline ...
we may overlook all
evidence divine.

Thought for the Day: We need to be reminded daily of God's love, and to do so, we need to look beyond the headlines of war and misery to the armies of charity and goodwill—God's witnesses.

SEPTEMBER 15

Scripture Reading: Psalm 84

Verse for the Day: "How lovely is your dwelling place, O Lord of hosts!" (Psalm 84:1)

Maybe a Mountain

Maybe a mountain
a desert place
a quiet room
a backyard space
a sandy beach
by a timeless sea
a city street
a big shade tree—
wherever you find
the time to praise
go often there
on busy days.
Let there be silence
so God can speak
to shatter doubt
for those who seek
to abandon guilt
relinguish pride
struggle for purpose
leave self aside
find assurance
through earnest prayer, of
divine compassion
and endless love.

Thought for the Day: Today I will find time to seek guidance and to praise God who will provide the strength and assurance I need.

SEPTEMBER 16

Scripture Reading: II Peter 3:14-18

Verse for the Day: "... beware that you are not carried away with the error of the lawless and lose your own stability." (II Peter 3:17b)

In Search of Stability

Lord, keep me on an even keel;
sometimes depression makes me feel
       that life is just too hard, and I
       will fail no matter what I try.

My sin, I know, is taking on
myself what should be yours alone
       and thinking that it all depends
       on me and just what fortune sends.

The fear and doubt and lack of trust
are real and harmful, and I must
       relinquish them as bids to dodge
       commitment through such camouflage.

I only need to keep my mind
and heart set on your will to find
       the even temper, patience, peace
       that cause my demon's thrust to cease.

Thought for the Day: Sometimes, when I'm tempted to think I can go it alone, events and circumstances overwhelm me. I need to be reminded every day that my stability rests in God.

SEPTEMBER 17

Scripture Reading: James 2:18-26

Verse for the Day: "For just as the body without the spirit is dead, so faith without works is also dead." (James 2:26)

About Lee

He lived just down the street,
       and yet we never knew
how hard things had become;
       we didn't have a clue.
He'd always lived alone;
       we saw him come and go,
yet, details of his life
       we really didn't know.
My neighbor just next door
       and I exchanged a "hi"
with him from time to time
       but weren't the types to pry.
We knew his name was Lee
       and that he didn't drive
but never thought to check
       if he were still alive.
They found him late one day;
       his cabinets were bare;
utilities cut off;
       house stifling with stale air.
Why had we failed to act?
       Why didn't someone see?
Lord, please don't deal with us
       as we had dealt with Lee.

Thought for the Day: Failure to be attentive to the needs of others can leave us filled with remorse, but we'll never have to feel guilty for being too kind.

SEPTEMBER 18

Scripture Reading: Mark 8:34-38

Verse for the Day: "For those who want to save their life will lose it, and those who lose their life for my sake, and for the sake of the gospel, will save it." (Mark 8:35)

Self-Preservation

If you feel a nervous breakdown coming on,
and you don't know how you'll manage all alone,
    just go out across the tracks,
    lift some loads from weary backs,
and you'll find your nerves are mending on their own.

If you feel time hanging heavy on your hands,
and your lonely self creates unreal demands,
    go find some who are oppressed,
    over-worked, and sore distressed,
and make helping them a part of each day's plans.

If you feel that life has been unfair to you,
and just hanging on is all that you can do,
    throw a portion of the rope
    to someone else who's needing hope,
and let helping him or her be your rescue.

Thought for the Day: Losing self in helping others is the surest way of saving one's life or preserving one's sanity. Nothing is as nerve-wracking, lonely, and life-demeaning as self-centeredness.

SEPTEMBER 19

Scripture Reading: Proverbs 27:1-11

Verse for the Day: "Better is a neighbor who is nearby than kindred who are far away." (Proverbs 27: 10b)

They Said

From distance they said I should sell and move;
that this place is too big since you are gone.
The lawn is growing up, but there's a groove
I've worn between the porch and your car on
the drive. I take it everywhere I go.
Seated in your car behind the wheel I
feel close to you. They wrote and said they know
what I am going through. I'm sure they try.

They said I ought to get rid of your car—
that mine was good, and I did not need two—
that one of them would take it. Now that's par
for the course, I'd say, since yours is the new.
What they don't know, no matter what they said,
is that when I'm where you were, you're not dead.

Thought for the Day: It's better not to make many immediate changes when there's been a death. Advisers mean well, but the familiar is more comforting. The heart will know when it's time to move on.

SEPTEMBER 20

Scripture Reading: Job 5:17-27

Verse for the Day: "How happy is the one whom God reproves; therefore do not despise the discipline of the Almighty." (Job 5:17)

The Rainbow

The rainbow in the sky
comes only when it rains;
the colors multiply
through water-prismed veins.

The pride in victory
grows after a defeat;
who've lost will all agree
loss makes the winning sweet.

The bliss when suffering's done
and gone is torment's strain
is only known by one
who has defeated pain.

And faith which stands the test
of trial through life's steep climb
is doctrine at its best
which won't expire with time.

Thought for the Day: There are rainy seasons of trial and defeat in every life, but these only make the rainbows seem more beautiful when they appear.

SEPTEMBER 21

Scripture Reading: Genesis 11:1-9

Verse for the Day: "Therefore it was called Babel, because there the Lord confused the language of all the earth, and from there the Lord scattered them abroad over the face of the earth." (Genesis 11:9)

Tower of Babel

The human condition is such
that we don't comprehend very much;
    we often don't hear
    or see through our fear,
and we try not ever to touch.

We don't consider it shame
not knowing our neighbor's name,
    for we have on TV
    a hundred channels to see,
and we're so busy playing the game.

We learn to speak only to hide
our true selves—we never confide;
    because if we did,
    our words would be pitted
against us and then be denied.

But God's reign is close when our ears
are unstopped, and our tongues loosed of fears;
    when revealing of truth
    won't be called uncouth
and is cause not for dread but for cheers!

Thought for the Day: When pride and self-acclaim threaten to separate us from humble acknowledgement that we need God, we face the predicament of estrangement from humanity as well.

SEPTEMBER 22

Scripture Reading: John 21:15-24

Verse for the Day: "Peter felt hurt because he said to him the third time, 'Do you love me?' And he said to him, 'Lord, you know that I love you.' Jesus said to him, 'Feed my sheep.'" (John 21:17b)

The Follow-Through

If you love me feed my lambs,
tend my sheep, feed them, too.
Christ was most insistent
in this matter for he knew
the tendency of people
to neglect the follow-through.

It's one thing to say we love,
quite another to commit
to tending and feeding.
We're inclined to forget
when things get harried,
or we see no benefit.

Lord, help me mean it when
I say my love is true.
For I know that good
intentions don't accrue
results. And only as I
serve others do I love you.

Thought for the Day: Good intentions don't feed the hungry or tend to the needs of those in trouble. I want to be counted among those who care enough to follow through.

SEPTEMBER 23

Scripture Reading: Ephesians 3:1-13

Verse for the Day: "... to make everyone see what is the plan of the mystery hidden for ages in God who created all things;" (Ephesians 3:9)

The Plan

God's plan, revealed in Christ,
was that all might believe
in love and selflessness
and beauty ... might receive
forgiveness for all sin,
a welcome to the fold,
a slate wiped clean again,
the courage to uphold
conviction of the right;
to stand against the wrong,
to live within the light,
to sing a joyful song.

Thought for the Day: I will remember today that God's plan is to cover the redemption and provide for the salvation of the whole world.

SEPTEMBER 24

Scripture Reading: I Samuel 3

Verse for the Day: "...'Speak, for your servant is listening.'" (I Samuel 3:10b)

God's Voice

Sometimes God's voice speaks through the still of
night;
sometimes through lightning strike in raging storm;
sometimes through sermon's reasoning insight
when suddenly the calloused heart grows warm.

In times past God's voice spoke from rolling cloud
or out of prairie bush with burst of flame;
at times the voice has seemed to speak out loud;
at times it's staked a silent, heart-felt claim.

A dream may stir the Spirit's vocal chords;
a prayerful vision may call forth the voice;
or even prison walls be sounding boards
for God to speak; creative force has choice.

Surprise will greet all those who truly seek ...
for God is limitless in ways to speak!

Thought for the Day: The still small voice within may be the way God reaches me, but someone else may need a flashier signal. The important thing is to be listening.

SEPTEMBER 25

Scripture Reading: Ecclesiastes 5:10-20

Verse for the Day: "The lover of money will not be satisfied with money, nor the lover of wealth, with gain. This also is vanity." (Ecclesiastes 5:10)

All Is Vanity

If it's money you crave
and over wealth you rave,
>   you'll never be satisfied.
For there isn't enough
of that precious green stuff
>   which many have deified.

The stocks and the bonds
are like magic wands
>   to those who think rapture lies
in the prospect of gold
and the power it holds ...
>   but are they in for surprise!

For it's all vanity;
watch closely—you'll see
>   that the real wealth is in faithfulness.
It's God's peace providing,
through God's love abiding,
>   God's power to heal and to bless.

Thought for the Day: If I've overlooked the obvious,that money and wealth do not make for happiness, I pray that today my eyes might be opened.

SEPTEMBER 26

Scripture Reading: Acts 2:22-28

Verse for the Day: "But God raised him up, having freed him from death, because it was impossible for him to be held in its power." (Acts 2:24)

Had the Stone Not Rolled Away

Had Christ not left the tomb
alive, crops that today
are vibrant with fresh bloom
would not react that way.
The earth, a garden fair,
in protest would have shrunk
to withered stalk in bare
unwatered, shriveled chunk
of dirt. The push of life
from in the seed had failed
and elements in strife
would have, by now, assailed
all living creatures, sad
and forced to face each day
afraid and furtive had
the stone not rolled away.

Thought for the Day: Perhaps, more often than once a year on Easter, we ought to contemplate the difference the resurrection makes in our lives.

SEPTEMBER 27

Scripture Reading: II Kings 4:1-17

Verse for the Day: "Since you have taken all this trouble for us, what may be done for you?" (II Kings 4:13a)

The Reward

Elisha, the prophet,
    a man of God—
wherever he went,
    whatever road trod—
was doing for others
    without thought of self,
unconscious of gain,
    of bounty or pelf.
The Shunammite woman
    was open to hear
the need of another,
    to see her way clear
to welcome the prophet,
    providing a bed;
though effort for her,
    she found pleasure instead.
The reward of her kindness—
    a wish fulfilled—
was received through God's word
    which the prophet instilled.
Though nothing expected
    for good deeds wrought,
we're often surprised
    what goodness has brought!

Thought for the Day: When we do good, expecting no reward, whatever happens will be rewarding, even if it's only the satisfaction of knowing we have done it.

SEPTEMBER 28

Scripture Reading: Hebrews 12:11-17

Verse for the Day: "Pursue peace with everyone, and the holiness without which no one will see the Lord." (Hebrews 12:14)

In Pursuit of Peace

If only she would forgive me!
Although I don't know what I've done,
I'd gladly acquiesce—agree—
whatever it is—she's won.
I just want her friendship again,
for things to be like they were.
We'd visit on the phone, and then
sometimes I'd share a poem with her.
Or she would read a morsel from
the story she was working on.
It's good to have a friend to come
by when you're feeling all alone.
I would apologize—but
I don't know what I'm sorry for.
One day when I called, she just cut
me off abruptly, and that door
has remained shut. When I see her
she's speaks—but rebuffs when I've dared
try to be a peace-maker
for war that's never been declared.

Thought for the Day: Holiness does not demand that every fracture be healed, every dispute be settled, but that the pursuit of peace and understanding be a life goal.

SEPTEMBER 29

Scripture Reading: Deuteronomy 26:1-5

Verse for the Day: "When you have come into the land that the Lord your God is giving you as an inheritance to possess, and you possess it, and settle in it ..." (Deuteronomy 26:1)

When, Not If

"When Johnny comes back home," she often said,
"we'll work to ease the pain from which he fled.
Whatever inner turmoil drove him away,
we'll somehow make it right on that day
      when Johnny comes back home."
For two years he'd been gone; at just sixteen
he ran away; caught somewhere in between
the child and the adult. Lost in limbo,
he felt escape the only way to go.
      For two years he'd been gone.
Like ancient Israelites, those stalwart souls
who thanked the Lord before they reached their goals,
Johnny's mother gained the power to cope
by daily searching God's word. She lived on hope;
      did not give way to dread.
Johnny's mother always said, not "if" but "when."
Things do not always work out as we plan; then
faith in God's design must be the cause for praise.
"God's mysterious ways are not our ways,"
      Johnny's mother always said.

Thought for the Day: Daily Bible reading and prayer will keep us close to God, so that even when our plans do not work out, we feel divine presence.

SEPTEMBER 30

Scripture Reading: Philippians 4:8-23

Verse for the Day: "Finally, beloved, whatever is true, whatever is honorable, whatever is just, whatever is pure, whatever is pleasing, whatever is commendable, if there is any excellence and if there is anything worthy of praise, think about these things." (Philippians 4:8)

Worthy of Praise

Lilting songs
clanging gongs
ringing bells
ocean swells
singing birds
stirring words
dancing toes
fancy bows.

Flashing light
out-of-sight
thumping heart
early start
twinkling eyes
starry skies
lush perfume
love in bloom!

Thought for the Day: Love is of God and worthy of praise. Only the best thoughts and most unselfish desires deserve to be in the company of love.

THE BETTER PART

October

OCTOBER 1

Scripture Reading: Luke 10:38-42

Verse for the Day: "Martha, Martha, you are worried and distracted by many things; there is need of only one thing. Mary has chosen the better part..." (Luke 10:41a-42b)

Distractions

So many voices
distracting my mind
tapping on my consciousness,
slipping up from behind.
I cannot rest,
relax, or unwind.

Worries for the future
hold me bound to stress.
Trying to focus
is utterly useless.
Then comes the thought: one thing
I have yet to possess.

Just one thing I need!
Why can't I get a hold on
the better portion
which the Lord has shown.
That part which Martha and I
should both have known.

Thought for the Day: When Jesus reminded Martha that her busyness was distracting her from the joy Mary had found, I'm sure he spoke to me, as well.

OCTOBER 2

Scripture Reading: Zephaniah 3:14-20

Verse for the Day: "I will save the lame and gather the outcast, and I will change their shame into praise and renown in all the earth." (Zephaniah 3:19b)

On the Board

"The Lord looks after the fools," she would say,
"so I know I'm being looked after today."
She gathered polk salad beside the road
and picked up branches till she had a load,
then made for home, an old tar-paper shack
under the viaduct down by the track.

"Used to be a teacher," she once noted
to a newspaper man and was quoted
as saying she lived where she did by choice—
that she wanted to give outcasts a voice.
So she showed up at city council meets
and spoke, when allowed, for those on the streets.

Burning the branches and cooking the polk,
she shared what she had with all sorts of folk.
She listened to what each one had to say—
was nobody's fool—this old cast-a-way.
And when up in heaven she meets the good Lord,
I'll bet she's invited to serve on the Board.

Thought for the Day: Those society looks upon as outcasts are just children of God with special needs, and how pleased the Lord must be when those needs are met.

OCTOBER 3

Scripture Reading: Genesis 4:8-16

Verse for the Day: "Am I my brother's keeper?" (Genesis 4:9b)

Am I?

Am I my brother's keeper?
Or my sister's; am I?
If so, what does that mean?
What must I do, and why?

I do not kill or maim
or even cheat my neighbor.
From giving charitably.
I do not shirk or waver.

I give old clothes to help
aid-shelters furnish things
for homeless folks to wear—
no thought of gain—no strings!

Though tax deduction's nice,
that surely doesn't mean
my gifts are unworthy
or my motives unclean.

But is there something else
that I must do or try
if I would follow Christ?
Yes, think of "our" not "my."

Thought for the Day: The answer to the question is "yes." We are our brother's and sister's keepers. And every child of God is our brother or sister.

OCTOBER 4

Scripture Reading: I Chronicles 16:23-34

Scripture Reading: "Oh give thanks to the Lord, for he is good, for his steadfast love endures forever." (I Chronicles 16:34)

God Is Good

The little seed
I plant today
lies buried in the ground,
but come next spring
it leaps to life
—skyward bound.

Day after day
the elements
provide the nourishment,
but elements
are just a name
for earth's care, heaven-sent.

It's God alone
who gives the seed
its springtime livelihood,
for God is just
another name
for all in life that's good.

Thought for the Day: God is so all-encompassing throughout life that it is no exaggeration to say that within divine providence we live and move and have our being.

OCTOBER 5

Scripture Reading: Romans 1:8-17

Verse for the Day: "... as it is written, 'The one who is righteous will live by faith.'" (Romans 1:17b)

Being "Big" About It!

"That's big of him!"
And what is meant
is that his actions
lifted spirits, sent
a signal that the good
of all is uppermost.

A person "big" in this way
wouldn't want to boast,
but putting others first
comes second nature to
a bona fide "big" soul.
(Of course, a few
use this phrase as
facetiousness;
"that's big of him"
then means much less.)

It has nothing to do with
size, but spirit. And
being "big" means
something grand.

Thought for the Day: Being a "big" person in this sense of the word is a noble goal to which any of us can aspire, referring, as it does, to moral not physical stature.

OCTOBER 6

Scripture Reading: Genesis 1:20-25

Verse for the Day: "And God said, 'Let the waters bring forth swarms of living creatures, and let birds fly above the earth across the dome of the sky.'" (Genesis 1:20)

Need to Fly

Into evening bliss
comes the cacophony of
"quack" and "honk"—a kiss
on wind as southward
bound the ducks and geese go by.
Fall's arrival heard!

As meditation
moment moves the soul to look up,
the bird oblation
fills the autumn sky
and stirs within the spirit
the ancient need to fly.

The same faith makes birds
head south when cold breath is felt
that is found in words
of Scripture which prod
their human counterparts to
go in search of God.

Thought for the Day: All living things are of God, with instincts toward self-preservation which pulls them in the right direction. For human beings that's toward the Creator.

OCTOBER 7

Scripture Reading: I Timothy 6:6-11

Verse for the Day: "Of course there is great gain in godliness combined with contentment." (I Timothy 6:6)

The Man on the Phone

I watched him from the car,
the man there on the phone.
He paced the length of cord
to which it seemed he'd grown.
He gestured with free hand
through air with fingers spread;
and then he'd rub his brow,
hand cradling his head.
He wasn't very tall
but sturdy and well-groomed;
nice looking, touch of gray—
but that phone call seemed doomed.
Whatever his plea was,
it was not well-received;
his sales pitch unrewarded;
his message not believed.
I wondered what he thought
as he walked to his car.
Did he have far to go?
Had he driven very far?
Oh, if we only knew
the troubles others face ...
we'd be more satisfied
with our own time and place.

Thought for the Day: I will appreciate my own set of circumstances, avoid envy, and give thanks today.

OCTOBER 8

Scripture Reading: Luke 12:54-59

Verse for the Day: "And why do you not judge for yourself what is right?" (Luke 12:57)

Even Now

The child with sad, brown eyes,
watched others play.
Approached by teacher, she replied
in broken speech—
"No understand; no can play,"
as if to say
I'm doomed to be alone;
no one will teach
me how to play the game
or how to fit
into this alien life.
Just when it seemed
the elfin waif was sure to be
a lone misfit,
a chubby little blonde girl—
like artist dreamed—
approached the child and took her hand.
"I'll teach you how,"
she said, and pulled her into play.
"Come on, you'll see."
The brown eyes lit like lightning strike.
And even now,
years later, I still feel that hand
offered to me.

Thought for the Day: Today I want to remember the kindness shown me through the years by people who did not have to be kind. Then, I want to do something for someone to show my gratitude.

OCTOBER 9

Scripture Reading: Deuteronomy 32:7-12

Verse for the Day: "Remember the days of old, consider the years long past..." (Deuteronomy 32:7a)

In Remembrance of Things Past

When I see white-faced Herefords in the field,
I am a child of eight or ten back on
the farm my grandfather tended; its yield,
for me, a collection from tribes long gone:
arrow heads and stone bowls and rock-hewn knives.
For next to pasture land were fields to plow,
and there, as furrows turned, the buried lives
of ancient peoples were unearthed. Somehow
I'm there again and play beside the fence,
be watched by solemn white-faced Hereford bull,
whose presence menaced my every move, since
he was vicious-looking and powerful.
        Today when I see fields where Herefords graze,
        I live again enchanted childhood days.

Thought for the Day: Many things serve as symbols to take us back to remembrances of things past. Such is the cross and the stained-glass window and the sacrament. Remembering is a big part of faith.

OCTOBER 10

Scripture Reading: Ecclesiastes 1:5-9

Verse for the Day: "What has been is what will be, and what has been done is what will be done; there is nothing new under the sun." (Ecclesiastes 1:9)

Nature's Way

October has come—
yellow, orange, red, and gold
October. The breeze
becomes a sharp hum
of winds—bold
and lethal—which seize
the landscape. The thumb
of winter has planted cold
seeds of quick freeze.

Then, a sudden numb
heat takes hold
again. And black bees
swarm—their nests of honey-gum
impacted in old,
long-suffering honey-trees.
Dog-days—quarrelsome,
roused, cajoled.
Nature is a tease!

Thought for the Day: Aware of the capricious bent of nature, yet knowing there's nothing new, we often take for granted its mystery, wonder, and beauty. If we do, it will wake us up!

OCTOBER 11

Scripture Reading: Hebrews 10:11-18

Verse for the Day: "... says the Lord: 'I will put my laws in their hearts, and I will smite them on their minds. I will remember their sins and their lawless deeds no more.'" (Hebrews 10:16b-17)

When ...

When God's great laws are written
in the heart and on the mind
of every earth inhabitant,
of all of humankind ...

then war and threat of war
will be forever in the past,
and songs of liberation
be the only sounds that last.

Sins and lawless deeds will be
remembered nevermore,
and stories in newspapers
recount tales of quaint folklore.

When God's great laws are written
not on tablets made of stone,
but in humanity ... then earth will be
a peaceful, hate-free zone.

Thought for the Day: Humankind's effort to thwart the will of God will ultimately be to no avail. The Lord is quite capable of working out divine purpose.

OCTOBER 12

Scripture Reading: Matthew 14:22-33

Verse for the Day: "Peter answered him, 'Lord if it is you, command me to come to you on the water.' He said, 'Come.'" (Matthew 14:28)

On the Lake

Out on the lake at evening time
the glimmer from the shore as lights
are lit in homes is cosmic rhyme
in poetry of autumn nights.

In poetry of autumn nights
the winds make riding waves sublime
as bouncing of the shoreline lights
accelerates the spirit's climb.

Somewhere in distance church bells chime
as rolling waves and bouncing lights
accelerate the spirit's climb
to rapturous, ecstatic heights.

In bells and wind and waves and lights
my pristine self engages prime,
rhythmic devices of delights
out on the lake at evening time.

Thought for the Day: Anywhere the forces of nature combine to propel the spirit upward, God is surely there. I will look for the divine wherever I am.

OCTOBER 13

Scripture Reading: Hosea 8:4-7

Verse for the Day: "... an artisan made it; it is not from God. For they sow the wind, and they shall reap the whirlwind." (Hosea 8:6a,7a)

Beware the Whirlwind

We do not worship golden calves
or figures made of clay;
we do not bend the knee before
altars where idols stay.

But still we reap the whirlwind of
corruption and deceit,
and everywhere we turn there's crime's
disruption in the street.

Could be our golden calves come in
the form of greed-sought gain;
could be we've knelt at feet of
violent gore, commercial pain.

It just could be we've deified
unworthy measuring rod.
Beware that what is man-made
does not become your God.

Thought for the Day: Every day I must be aware of the temptation to find something more exciting, more sensational, more worldly to worship than the steadfast, slow to anger Almighty God.

OCTOBER 14

Scripture Reading: Luke 12:22-43

Verse for the Day: "Do not be afraid, little flock, for it is your Father's good pleasure to give you the kingdom." (Luke 12:32)

Come, Let Me Tell You

Come and let me tell you something—
　　　　something you might never hear of
if I did not share the secret
　　　　I have learned accepting God's love.
It's the secret of a living
　　　　free of guilt and free of losing,
free of anguish—always wanting
　　　　more and more of my own choosing.
It's the secret of surrender—
　　　　not a giving up of power,
rather an envelopment of
　　　　holy benefits each hour.
Thus, surrounded by such goodness,
　　　　strengthened in God's will, and waiting
always for Creation's impulse—
　　　　I have found all fear abating.
Unafraid, I need not struggle,
　　　　making enemies of others—
unafraid, I can acknowledge
　　　　sisterhood with all earth brothers.

Thought for the Day: To be free of guilty feelings and fearful thoughts is the most blessed state of living, and only in God's love can such freedom be achieved.

OCTOBER 15

Scripture Reading: Psalm 145:10-13

Verse for the Day: "All your works shall give thanks to you, O God." (Psalm 145:l0a)

For This Reason

In autumn when the leaves begin to fall,
I think I like this season best of all;
reminded of the days I went to school;
the season that King Football gets to rule.

The pompoms, black and gold or red and white;
the huddled comfort of the crowded night
in stadium of shared dreams born of youth,
where win or lose was temporary truth.

When trees are bare and vision simplified,
the distance seen without a place to hide,
I wade brown, brittle leaves in dusty trance
remembering the crush of sophomore dance.

Ready or not, here comes the winter chill.
It always comes; I'm sure it always will.
But not before God's splendid autumn starts
rejuvenating worn, time-jaded hearts.

Thought for the Day: Seasons have their reasons. God's plan for this world is not always discernable, but it is always God's plan, and I fit in it. It's up to me to discover how.

OCTOBER 16

Scripture Reading: Isaiah 30:15-18

Verse for the Day: "For thus says the Lord God, the holy one of Israel, 'In returning and rest you shall be saved; in quietness and in trust shall be your strength.'" (Isaiah 30:15)

In the End

Men and women, girls and boys,
in search of thrills and temporal joys,
refuse to see in cosmic beauty
love and peace and wealth a-plenty ...

thrusting thenceforth for the money
miss the beehive brimming honey;
never pausing in reflection
of a child's designed perfection ...

seeking constantly for pleasure
overlook the bubbling treasure—
water pure from deep, hot fountain
flowing from the mighty mountain.

Those who would be rich in excess
find that in the end they have less
than the ones who've understood
heaven and earth and personhood.

Thought for the Day: This day I want to be still long enough to look with seeing eyes upon the world and those about me in the light of gratitude to God.

OCTOBER 17

Scripture Reading: Matthew 5:33-37

Verse for the Day: "Let your 'Yes' be 'Yes' and your 'No,' 'No.'" (Matthew 5:37)

The Word of Truth

"There is no need to swear," he'd say.
A man of truth, there was no way
he'd ever lie, distort, evade,
or slant the facts by points not made.

His life was truth. He was well known
as a man of his word, one who'd grown
with the reputation—deserved—
of telling the truth; never swerved

by pressures to bend with the breeze—
tell half-truths or make up with ease
tall tales of sheer fabrication
or mislead with deliberation.

"Let yes be yes and no be no,"
he'd tell his children even though
he knew that they instinctively
saw nothing yet by honesty.

And they never learned to deceive
from father they could not believe.
What he told them, they knew was so—
his yes was yes; his no meant no.

Thought for the Day: Children learn best by example. Today I will make my life such that any child who might be watching will learn only the truth.

OCTOBER 18

Scripture Reading: Romans 1:16-21

Verse for the Day: "Ever since the creation of the world his eternal power and divine nature, invisible though they are, have been understood and seen through the things he has made." (Romans 1:20a)

Evidence A-Plenty

This morning I walked to the mailbox;
the sun coming up on the lake
reflected on frost-dampened leaf bed
and startled the snow birds awake.

Predictions of snow in the forecast
make children who wait for the bus
think longingly of school's dismissal,
and watch for the clouds—cumulus.

I, too, like the snow, and I look for
the first fall of flakes through the air;
the blanketed lawn in the evening—
the unchallenged purity there.

God speaks through creation continued.
each season's dawn testifies
that still and forever God's hand moves
throughout earth, on seas, and in skies.

Thought for the Day: God can be seen in the season's first snowfall as surely as in the new beds of spring. There is no shortage of evidence of continuing creation.

OCTOBER 19

Scripture Reading: Psalm 90

Verse for the Day: "So teach us to count our days that we may gain a wise heart. Let the favor of the Lord our God be upon us and prosper for us the work of our hands." (Psalm 90:12,17)

Give It a Try

When the heart has been overburdened
and enough tears shed to flood the sea,
what do folks do who have nobody ...
if they have not love of poetry?

Poems can touch the heart as nothing else.
be company to newly grieving
who cannot reach out to any friend
or keep the next of kin from leaving.

Psalms are poems: much of Solomon's Song;
and poems are found on other pages
of Scripture. What do those folks do
who get no help from poetic sages?

A poem is the song of heart to heart;
good poetry has music in it.
When heartache threatens to engulf, spend
an hour with poetry in each minute.

Thought for the Day: Meditation, with the help of poetry, is one path to divine inspiration. Like prayer and the sacraments, a good poem is touched by God.

OCTOBER 20

Scripture Reading: Job 42:1-6, 10-17

Verse for the Day: "Then Job answered the Lord: 'I know that you can do all things, and that no purpose of yours can be thwarted. I had heard of you by the hearing of the ear, but now my eye sees you.'" (Job 42: 1-2,5)

With Eye on the Goal

A happy ending is not always possible,
but resting on God's promises through pain
is the prescription for a life of certainty
that sometime soon the sun will shine again.

When neighbors wondered why Job did not curse the Lord
and die in order to escape the blight
that settled on his life and dealt such misery,
they did not understand that God was light

through which Job saw that all his grief was temporal—
a bane that could not banish steadfast soul.
A man of faith, Job recognized that God alone
was his salvation and his spirit's goal.

Thought for the Day: Sometimes there seems no rationale for troubles which appear random and purposeless. But God's overarching intention for our lives has purpose. We were made for divine fellowship.

OCTOBER 21

Scripture Reading: Galatians 6:1-6

Verse for the Day: "Bear one another's burdens, and in this way you will fulfill the law of Christ." (Galatians 6:2)

Lesson Unlearned

"I've got trouble of my own,"
the old man often complained;
"I can't worry about others
who ought to be restrained
from asking for help—they need to work!
I've too much trouble of my own."

Sure enough, he's had some trouble—
his wife left him all alone
(told others he was stingy, mean,
and angry all the time).
His employees strike each year; claim
he hates parting with a dime.
His neighbors hardly ever speak;
they long ago had learned,
that any attempt at friendship
would be callously spurned.

Trouble should make one sensitive;
he got more hateful and gruff.
Instead of too much trouble,
maybe he's not had enough.

Thought for the Day: Even in the darkest of times, I must never be so self-absorbed that I fail to be aware of and responsive to the needs of others.

OCTOBER 22

Scripture Reading: Psalm 111

Verse for the Day: "Great are the works of the Lord, studied by all who delight in them." (Psalm 111:2)

Pat

She smiled—the sweetest smile I'd ever seen.
Her brow knit with compassion as she said,
"I'll take you back to where he lies." Between
the desks, we walked through hall to table-bed
in sterile room where tubes and bandages
engulfed the tiny figure sound asleep.
"His recovery will come in stages ..."
her voice was soft, and I began to weep
as she added, tenderly, "... if at all."
She wanted to prepare me for the worst.
I sat for days, nearby against the wall,
so when that faint "yip" sounded, I was first
to hear. Then watched, as with a yelping wheeze
life stirred in Pat, my precious Pekinese.

Thought for the Day: Pets are dear to those who live alone or to any who need the companionship and unconditional love they provide. I will be thoughtful of all animals as God's creatures.

OCTOBER 23

Scripture Reading: Hebrews 11:1-16

Verse for the Day: "Now faith is the assurance of things hoped for, the conviction of things not seen." (Hebrews 11:1)

The Only Thing We've Got

A sure thing? No.
But what is?
Faith is all we've got.
That faith looks like
a question mark
puzzles us a lot.

But still and all
it's better
than living as a blot.
At least we can
stand firm on
that substantial dot!

Thought for the Day: There is very little in life that is absolutely certain. Faith in people and things is often misplaced. What, then, is there but faith in God?

OCTOBER 24

Scripture Reading: Amos 5:6-7, 10-15

Verse for the Day: "Hate evil and love good, and establish justice in the gate." (Amos 5:15a)

Amos

The faithful prophet in a wicked age
comes alive today on the Scripture page.
The words seem downright contemporary
with faithless living and ways contrary
to God's most righteous generosity.
Presumptuous pride brings calamity,
depriving the poor of justice in court.
The rich taking bribes as evil's consort,
seeing themselves as put upon and used—
not recognizing privilege abused.

Old Amos still speaks to make us aware
that God's word is truth, and judgment is there.

Thought for the Day: Judgment is not something we like to think about, but it's something we can't escape. For the Christian the harshest judgment is a sensitive conscience.

OCTOBER 25

Scripture Reading: Matthew 6:7-13

Verse for the Day: "Pray then in this way: Our Father in heaven, hallowed be your name. Your kingdom come. Your will be done, on earth as it is in heaven." (Matthew 6:9-10)

All or Nothing at All

I do not know a lot of things,
like why the wind whips like a dart
through storm clouds moving overhead,
or why some say that God is dead.
Nor why the dying thornbird sings.
I know not why great city's heart
was wracked with pain that will not cease—
or if there ever will be peace.
I do not know if time will come
when lion will lay down with lamb,
or when the color of one's skin
will not determine "who fits in."
Though tempting, I shall not succumb
to second guess the great "I AM."
And yet, sometimes I think I know.

When venon spews across the air,
and hate is practiced as an art,
there can be no security
for presidents ... or you, or me.
If this one fragile, floating globe
is where all life must share the loss or gain,
can we not learn that what hurts one
leaves all the world in terminal pain?

Thought for the Day: "Your will be done on earth as it is in heaven." Surely there's no hate there!

318

OCTOBER 26

Scripture Reading: Hebrews 6:1-12

Verse for the Day: "For God is not unjust; he will not overlook your work and the love that you showed for his sake in serving the saints, as you still do." (Hebrews 6:10)

The Future Is Now

"I don't need any test!"
Cantankerous and scared,
she balked at entering
the door behind which blared
intercom instructions for Dr. Anderson.
"But Mom, your doctor says
this test needs to be done."
"He just wants the money,"
she snapped. "I want to go
home." But home had become
the place she used to know.
"I'll go live with my dad!"
"Mom, he died years ago."
"Well, my mama is still ..."
"No, Mother, she's gone. So,
now you need to come on
and get this test." Unsure
and doubting our motives
she just had to endure
what could not be refused.
Lord, help me always see
myself in her ... and know
someday this could be me.

Thought for the Day: "No one is an island," wrote John Donne. We're all a part of the whole, and one way or the other, how we treat others is decisive in determining our future.

OCTOBER 27

Scripture Reading: II Corinthians 4:1-6

Verse for the Day: "For it is the God who said, 'Let light shine out of darkness,' who has shone in our hearts to give the light of the knowledge of the glory of God in the face of Jesus Christ." (II Corinthians 4:6)

In an Instant

God, help us grow beyond
the narrow earth,
the low-hung sky,
the human soul from birth
too inward-bound
too slow to comprehend
the vastness of your love.
Oh, Lord, please send
that vision which
reveals earth as just
a stepping stone,
the sky as angel dust,
the soul as bigger
than life itself.
Creator, lift us
from the shelf
of self-absorption
and complacency
into that instant
of transcendency.

Thought for the Day: We must remember to give thanks for the radiant light from moments of divine contact. May they remain with us through the experiences of every day.

OCTOBER 28

Scripture Reading: Luke 18:5-17

Verse for the Day: "Let the children come to me, and do not stop them; for it is to such as these that the kingdom of God belongs." (Luke 18:16b)

In Magic Canyon

Magic Canyon it was called.
But there, that day, the "magic" was all gone.
The carousel still went around;
an organ played an organ sound,
but life seemed to be stalled.
As if in time-warp, living there went on.

It was after school started.
There's nothing "magic" about a theme park
with no children anywhere—
just adults with patient stare,
trying to assume light-hearted
pose or whip up a dormant, fun-fanned spark.

It was in a canyon, true,
and there were clowns, balloons, and treats to stuff.
But something there will always be
that doesn't like a park child-free.
No matter what the grown-ups do,
till kids come back, it will not be enough.

Thought for the Day: It's hard to imagine a world without children. Today, I will be especially careful to express my appreciation for the vitality children bring to life.

OCTOBER 29

Scripture Reading: Luke 18:9-17

Verse for the Day: "God, be merciful to me, a sinner!" (Luke 18:13b)

As God Sees

Once I caught sight of just how I must look
to God who views humanity in light
of Jesus Christ. I knew then what it took
to love and to forgive the selfish, trite,
unlovely souls with whom I deal each day:
the neighbor whose dog barks at night when I
need sleep; the co-worker who wants his way;
the slothful clerk who makes me wait. I'll try
to see in spiteful kin that which I hope
the Lord still sees in me—a soul in need
of friendship on sublimely hallowed scope.
And I shall follow where God's grace will lead.
      Until I reach perfection in the whole,
      I'll make forgiving others my main goal.

Thought for the Day: To see ourselves as others see us, someone has said, would be a freeing experience. To see ourselves as God sees us, would make us indebted forever to divine forgiveness.

OCTOBER 30

Scripture Reading: Ephesians 5:6-21

Verse for the Day: "Live as children of light, for the fruit of light is found in all that is good and right and true." (Ephesians 5:8b-9)

Winter Flowers

A snap to grow in the cold, so we're told,
as summertime flowers fade. Oh, to trade
months without flowers for a quaint bouquet—
purple, pink, yellow, white, blue, and red, too,
orange and black for Halloween! Well, I mean
who wouldn't trade? After freeze these pansies,
revive, velvet-textured, head up—not dead—
some solid, some with faces, and traces
of blended shades, size-varied. When carried
to the sick as small nosegay or made a
centerpiece for set table, they're able
to brighten the winter's chill. It's God's will.

Thought for the Day: Like the pansy, I should try to be a winter flower, bringing light and color to the world when all seems unproductive, forlorn, and cold. It's God's will.

OCTOBER 31

Scripture Reading: II Kings 2:1-15

Verse for the Day: "Elisha said, 'Please, let me inherit a double share of your spirit.' He [Elijah] responded, 'You have asked a hard thing.'" (II Kings 2:9b-10a)

A Hard Thing

The spirit of the prophet:
not perfection,
but devotion.

The inheritance:
not material,
but ethereal.

A double share:
not of recognition,
but of obligation.

The chariot:
not a cozy chaise,
but a fiery blaze.

Thought for the Day: There is no easy road promised for the faithful, just guidance and comfort and salvation.

WHERE PRAISES BELONG

November

NOVEMBER 1

Scripture Reading: Psalm 96

Verse for the Day: "O sing to the Lord a new song; sing to the Lord all the earth." (Psalm 96:1)

Where Praises Belong

A song of Thanksgiving!
O come let us sing ...
of bountiful land,
of birds on the wing,
of mountain trails winding,
of wild eagles' flight,
of soft sandy beaches,
sea gulls gleaming white.

A song of thanksgiving
for table well-spread ...
for turkey and dressing,
sweet peas, and fresh bread.
With thanksgiving let there
be voices in song
raised to the Creator,
where praises belong.

Thought for the Day: Every day should be a song of praise and thanksgiving for there is so much to praise and so much to be thankful for that it would take 365 days each year.

NOVEMBER 2

Scripture Reading: Ephesians 4:17-23

Verse for the Day: "... be renewed in the spirit of your minds, and clothe yourselves with the new self, created according to the likeness of God in true righteousness and holiness." (Ephesians 4:22)

November

November—such a pretty name
for such uncertainty.
Some days summer. Some days autumn.
Some, real wintery.

The perfect time for inventory
which just might reveal
that, as with old November,
our lives at times conceal
a panoply of mixed emotions—
responses, right and wrong.
Like November we're uncertain
just where we belong.

But life is just as beautiful
as November's name—
mercurial nature wonderful,
not a cause for shame.

Thought for the Day: Life is a series of ups and downs, good and bad, sunshine and rain. Months like November remind us that whatever yesterday brought, today is another day.

NOVEMBER 3

Scripture Reading: I Kings 8:37-40

Verse for the Day: "... then hear in heaven your dwelling place, forgive, act, and render to all whose hearts you know, according to all their way, for only you know what is in every human heart ..." (I Kings 8:39)

From the Sound

A sound has a life of its own:
the crunch of a crisp apple bitten,
the bell buoy out from the shore,
the whining of a newborn kitten.
the ring of a phone in the night,
the sizzle of oil for the sauce
when into hot skillet tomatoes
and onions and peppers are tossed ...
the rain falling hard on the barn's
roof of tin, and from damp-smelling hay
the giggles of children who take
refuge there but continue to play ...
the "whoosh" as the Greyhound's big door
hydraulically opens and closes,
the rapid retort of gunfire,
the death-scream its sounding imposes.
> From deep in the soul comes the sense
> that, triggered by some sudden sound,
> the secret to how we became
> what we are now might be found.

Thought for the Day: The thing we often overlook about God is the divine understanding of "why" we do what we do, "how" we became what we are, and "what" influences our response.

NOVEMBER 4

Scripture Reading: Acts 6:8-15

Verse for the Day: "And all who sat in the council, looking steadfastly at him, saw his face as the face of an angel." (Acts 6:15)

Face of an Angel

The Christian doesn't have to wear
    a face of "happy mask."
The radiance reflected there
    is not from duty's task.
The issue is not some pretense
    at joy while hiding tears,
but rather of God's glory shone
    through mortal pain and fears.
Those men who watched the martyrdom
    of Stephen knew that he
was somehow in the hand of God
    though death came cruelly.
An angel's face they said of him,
    divine the being shone.
It served to move stout-hearted Saul,
    who watched the hurl of stone.
Becoming Paul, new man, new name,
    he learned what Stephen knew.
I think he then and there acquired
    angelic features, too.
Who in our lives would come to know
    the Lord through face of ours?
Does my demeanor, day by day,
    reflect God's mighty powers?

Thought for the Day: No one should have to identify himself or herself as a Christian; that fact ought to be written on the face.

NOVEMBER 5

Scripture Reading: Job 22:21-28

Verse for the Day: "Agree with God and be at peace, in this way, good will come to you." (Job 22:21)

Patchwork Quilt

My life's a patchwork quilt cut out with care;
the pieces sewn in place with joy and tears.
Each block is testament to answered prayer.

When pillowed by deception and despair,
I know my comfort covers dreadful fears ...
brings light and color, sunshine's buoyant flair.

When strained relationships require repair,
a picture in the pattern-work appears ...
each block evokes an ambience to share.

When I have tried; met failure everywhere,
this undisputable, clear fact appears ...
my quilt tells tales of fortitude and dare.

When happiness has let me "walk on air,"
I reaffirm the truth of quilted years ...
that nothing leaves the Godly soul threadbare.

If triumph rule or tragedy ensnare,
I visualize the whole as heaven nears.
My life's a patchwork quilt cut out with care;
each block is testament to answered prayer.

Thought for the Day: The big picture requires that we see our lives as a network of inter-stitched experiences ... each a block in the quilt of life that will finally cover us.

NOVEMBER 6

Scripture Reading: Matthew 10:16-42

Verse for the Day: "When they hand you over, do not worry about how you are to speak or what you are to say; for what you are to say will be given to you at that time." (Matthew 10:19)

Always Prepared

Some seem to be never at a loss
    for words to say;
so glib and confident and secure;
    while I just pray
not to appear tongue-tied when unprepared
    for encounters.
I stutter and stammer, uttering
    some cat-like purrs
between words, in verbally pausing
    to clear my thought.
I wish I could think when unprepared,
    but I'm untaught
in skills of debate. If only I
    could learn to trust
that God would not desert me, but would
    use the dull dust
of my thinking to fashion worthwhile
    responses to
whatever challenges I should meet.
    For it is true!

Thought for the Day: Not many of us are always ready to take on a verbal challenge or maintain our cool when confronted, but sometimes silence, through which God can speak, is best.

NOVEMBER 7

Scripture Reading: James 2:12-17

Verse for the Day: "For judgment will be without mercy to anyone who has shown no mercy; mercy triumphs over judgment." (James 2:13)

Judgment Without Mercy

"No one listens to me," she complained.
      It was true. We turned her off
because she never had a good word
      to relate. She'd always scoff
at anyone who tried to brighten
      the mood or conversation.
Harsh judgment was her trademark, and so
      often her one oblation
was of censorship focused on those
      not present or able to
defend themselves. Simple mercy was
      not within her cold, shrewd stew
of devilment, hate, and poisonous
      personality. But, then
she knew we did not heed her sharp and
      biting criticisms when,
with focused venom, she would complain,
      "Nobody listens to me."
We knew that, if not around, we'd be
      the subject of her spree
of malice. Oh, how crucial is the
      lesson she missed. That mercy
is God's love in action and the key
      to heaven's door eventually.

Thought for the Day: Oh, let me learn the lesson well that those who constantly criticize and censor will miss the mercy they themselves do not extend.

NOVEMBER 8

Scripture Reading: I Corinthians 12:1-31

Verse for the Day: "To each is given the manifestation of the Spirit for the common good." (I Corinthians 12:7)

A Little Strange

She is a friend to animals.
Her next door neighbor said,
"Don't these pesky squirrels just drive you
wild?" She just shook her head,
then confessed, "Oh no, I feed them."
Several times a day
she throws peanuts out the back door.
She has a special way
of making conversation with
the redbird and racoon.
She calls her backyard friends "livestock;"
they recognize her tune
as she sings out, "Come on, come on!"
The chipmunk gets so bold
he climbs on her lap and lets
her stroke his back and hold
him while he gnaws on a peanut.
The birds and squirrels come
right up to the patio door—
beg for nut or bread crumb.
The neighbors think of her as "strange;"
without a doubt, it's true.
But "strange" is not a bad thing if
your friends can count on you.

Thought for the Day: Everyone has some special gift; maybe something as unusual as comraderie with the animals. But God entrusted all of us with something to contribute.

NOVEMBER 9

Scripture Reading: Genesis 15:1-21

Verse for the Day: "And he believed the Lord; and the Lord reckoned it to him as righteousness." (Genesis 15:6)

No Substitute

Insecurity, anxiety, fear,
emotional frustration, unrelieved stress,
lack of fulfillment year after year,
unsatisfied hunger, and loneliness ...
all names to call that inbred inner quest
to have relationship with God, for which
we're born and through which we're routinely blest.
We try to fill the dry and dusty ditch
with waters other than the living kind.
But substitutes will prove of no avail.
The longed-for solace and the peace of mind
is not found independent of the Holy Grail.

Our faith will fashion passage, through God's will,
to promised "balm"... embodied "peace be still."

Thought for the Day: Genuine faith in God is what counts as righteousness. Nothing will substitute, and God knows if our faith is genuine. We know, too, because that alone produces peace.

NOVEMBER 10

Scripture Reading: Revelation 21:1-6

Verse for the Day: "See I am making all things new." (Revelation 21:5)

The Visionary

Saints share a perception
of people as perfectible ...
plant seeds of a vision
in all those susceptible
to ideas of a new heaven and earth;
all things made new—all people, too.

Saints are not pure and perfect souls
with lives untouched by sin.
They simply labor hard to bring
a new Jerusalem in.

Saints care for individuals;
not just the world at large,
but hungry, lonely, fractured ones.
Each in need is the saint's charge.

Saints know that where there is no sight,
no vision to instill
the promise of a better world
the people always will
perish. The saint has sight to see
that, through it all, God's able;
that good will conquer evil,
and that souls are renewable.

Thought for the Day: Saints are simply people wholly dedicated to the idea that the earth and all its people belong to God and can be renewed with God's spirit and their help.

NOVEMBER 11

Scripture Reading: II Corinthians 3:2-4:6

Verse for the Day: "And all of us, with unveiled faces, seeing the glory of the Lord as though reflected in a mirror, are being transformed into the same image from one degree of glory to another; for this comes from the Lord, the Spirit." (II Corinthians 3:18)

The Likeness

I think that I shall someday be
the person I would like to see
when I look in the mirror here.
    I now see imaged, oh so clear,
    a work in progress, grown each day
    a little closer to the way
    God meant for each of us to be;
    but still unfinished, all agree
    who know me well and know that I
    fall way short even when I try.
Perhaps it's only deep inside
where I know God has often tried
to speak to me, that I sense grace—
but soon it will appear on face
which stares at me from mirrored walls.
    This longing for perfection calls,
    and only those who will believe
    that saints are what God can achieve
    with lives creatively turned toward
    the likeness of the living Lord,
    will ever actually see
    the persons we were meant to be.

Thought for the Day: Saints probably didn't set out to be saints, but rather to obey the Lord. In so doing they grew into the likeness of God in spirit.

NOVEMBER 12

Scripture Reading: Genesis 37:1-36

Verse for the Day: "Here comes this dreamer." (Genesis 37:19b)

Hold Fast

The difficulties Joseph met
would seem the end of any
hope for his dreams coming true.
The obstacles were many:

the hatred of his brothers,
the pit where he was thrown,
the trek to Egypt as a slave,
the lies about him sown.

But God had plans for Joseph
which circumstances stalled
but could not ultimately thwart
though tangled and embroiled.

He rose to a place of power,
a source of blessing to those
whom God would save through Egypt
before the chapter's close.

The lesson is for you and me—
hold fast to dreams God-given.
The route which seems most burdensome
may be the road to heaven.

Thought for the Day: Joseph became an instrument for God's purposes because he did not let circumstances defeat him. His life should serve as an example to us.

NOVEMBER 13

Scripture Reading: John 17:20-26

Verse for the Day: "... that they may all be one. As you, Father, are in me and I am in you, may they also be in us, so that the world may believe that you sent me." (John 17:21)

As Seen in the Parent

He looked through the box in his lap:
old pictures, a cracked shaving mug,
a yellowed, much used, U.S. map,
the watch that gave Mom's wrist a hug.

Then, filing through photos of past:
the first fishing trip with his dad,
the Christmas that was Granny's last,
the bell-bottoms when they were fad.

He sat for awhile deep in thought;
tears spattered the deed to the place,
which, early on, his folks had bought.
The sale—he now had to face.

Years passed and age had come on,
he'd grown like his dad in his ways;
yet, after his mother was gone,
he'd seen her in the glass some days.

Today as he handled the past,
he reflected on how he was blest
by parents who loved and held fast
the precepts of life at its best.

Thought for the Day: We give thanks for parents who instill love and Godly virtues, as filled the life of Christ, and for children who embody such ideals.

NOVEMBER 14

Scripture Reading: I Chronicles 29:10-13

Verse for the Day: "And now, our God, we give thanks to you and praise your glorious name." (I Chronicles 29:13)

Give Thanks, Then

Give thanks, then, for dreams,
  phantasmal designs, imaginings;
for crystal-pond reflections,
  tumbling weeds, and high-strung swings.
Give thanks for days to look back on
  with pleasure, for moments when
the pastures were peaceful
  and momentum was skyward, and then
be thankful for life, the gate
  which was opened, and time—
embraceable enemy, beloved thief,
  escapee extraordinaire, and healer sublime.
But, above all else, be thankful
  for faith in a deific scheme
where dying is, by design, restorative,
  and death a fantastic dream.

Thought for the Day: In the bigger scheme of things, if we could see from that perspective, birth, life, living, dying, death are parts of an awesome plan. We should feel grateful to be included.

NOVEMBER 15

Scripture Reading: Genesis 13:1-18

Verse for the Day: "Rise up, walk through the length and breadth of the land, for I will give it to you." (Genesis 13:17)

To Doubt or Not to Doubt?

To you who could not cause one leaf to grow,
or make one tree to flame in autumn light,
who could not place a star or even sow
a mountain which would spring to wondrous height;
you, who are bound to earth by breath of air,
who could not live elsewhere unless capsuled,
who could not make a cloudy day more fair,
or recreate one prismed crystal, jeweled
snowflake, blade of grass, or harvest moon;
to you who cannot calm destructive wind,
or turn the dark to day, or mark high noon,
or cause one broken bone to start to mend—
I'd caution spending too much time in doubt
of One who brings all this and more about.

Thought for the Day: The earth from the beginning was a gift. Doubts about God are inevitable, but the evidence—to the believer—is overwhelming.

NOVEMBER 16

Scripture Reading: Judges 6:1-35

Verse for the Day: "So they said to one another, 'Who did this thing?' After searching they were told, 'Gideon, son of Joash, did it.'" (Judges 6:29)

No Limit

There is no limit
to what God can do
with lives devoted
and directed to
fulfilling the goal
of the reign of God
in human affairs
where only a nod
toward divinity
has been the rule,
or where false Gods of
some alien school
have become enshrined.

Like young Gideon,
who tore down the Baal—
stood stalwart and won,
whoever is moved,
by soul stirred within,
to battle for right
will finally win.

Thought for the Day: There is no limit to what God can accomplish through individuals when the divine will becomes the guiding light.

NOVEMBER 17

Scripture Reading: I John 2:20-29

Verse for the Day: "As for you, the anointing that you received from him abides in you ..." (I John 2:27a)

The Anointed

I did not comprehend
the lesson as taught;
it was quite clear to you,
but I am so slow.

But then when you came
to see me you brought
a sense of the Savior ...
and now I know.

From your eyes I saw
Christ's welcome and grace;
from your heart his love
was abundantly shed.

In the depth of the smile
which lighted your face,
I lost sight of you—
saw Christ instead.

Thought for the Day: Others may see in us lessons that cannot be taught verbally. The smile, the gesture, the genuine concern speak louder than words.

NOVEMBER 18

Scripture Reading: Mark 11:20-26

Verse for the Day: "Whenever you stand praying, forgive, if you have anything against anyone; so that your Father in heaven may also forgive you your trespasses." (Mark 11:25-26)

Or Else

I found it very difficult
to forgive the one
who threatened my security;
left me trusting none.

She lied, and some believed her lies;
and I had to defend
myself against unfounded charge
that truth could not rescind.

Once spoken, words are always there,
no matter what effect;
and those which damage cannot be
recalled in retrospect.

But still, I knew I must forgive
for often I've trespassed;
and I need, more than any, God's
forgiveness at the last.

Thought for the Day: Forgiving is not so difficult, if first we list all the things in life for which we've needed to be forgiven.

NOVEMBER 19

Scripture Reading: II John 1-6

Verse for the Day: "And this is love, that we walk according to his commandments; this is the commandment just as you have heard it from the beginning, you must walk in it. (II John 6)

Friendship

Big parade
bold brass band,
water clear
by pure, white sand,
jet stream streak
above the land,
you and I
walk hand in hand.

Dinner meeting
just as planned,
scary movie
at the Strand,
stroll at sunset
weather grand,
you and I
walk hand in hand.

Thought for the Day: Friendship is made up of many little things shared. If there are enough of these little things, it stands the test of time.

NOVEMBER 20

Scripture Reading: Romans 16:25-27

Verse for the Day: "Now to God who is able to strengthen you according to my gospel ..." (Romans 16:25a)

My Gospel

I've had my share of messages
that left me in a stew ...
not knowing whether I could cope,
uncertain what to do.

I've also had some devastating
news that caused real grief.
I've lived through crises that were not
mitigatingly brief.

But always I have held on to
my gospel at its core—
the truth that God has for creation
better things in store.

I must believe that in this faith
God's great good news will quell
my anguish if I live and breathe
and **be** a living gospel.

Thought for the Day: Biblical passages must become lifestyle through experience until the good news is an integral part of who we are. This is the word incarnate.

NOVEMBER 21

Scripture Reading: Psalm 18:32-50

Verse for the Day: "You have given me the shield of your salvation, and your right hand has supported me; your help has made me great." (Psalm 18:35)

Living Thanksgiving

One day each year that's set aside
for giving thanks to God
seems extremely insufficient
and just a little odd.

What with all the days we're given—
three-hundred-sixty-five—
in which to profit from God's blessings,
to hoard earth's gifts, to thrive ...

we probably should think less of
Thanksgiving Holiday ...
instead, put daily effort in
thanks-living all the way.

Appreciation of God's grace,
aligned with gentle heart,
brings to life that spirit which is
heaven's earthly part.

Thought for the Day: Greatness in God's sight is found in humility and comes about through gratitude, which is, in genuine form, a daily exercise.

NOVEMBER 22

Scripture Reading: Acts 27:13-44

Verse for the Day: "Fearing that we might run on the rocks, they let down four anchors from the stern and prayed for day to come." (Acts 27:29)

Four Anchors

Four anchors should maintain the soul:
purpose, devotion, trust, and hope ...
Or else what reams through rain-dashed dreams
leaves us unable just to cope.

What are the anchors of my soul?
Through winds of doubt what fixes my
security and lets me see
tomorrow and a sun-filled sky?

When sorrow's tossing sea takes toll
and drowning seems the only course,
what plank would I grasp floating by?
What would be my salvation's source?

Four anchors then should steady me:
hope, trust, devotion, purpose, too.
For what controls as storm cloud rolls
is that which marks what I hold true.

Thought for the Day: It's not the calm sea or quiet port that tests what we believe. It's what happens to us in the storm that demonstrates our faith.

NOVEMBER 23

Scripture Reading: I Samuel 1:4-20

Verse for the Day: "And she said, 'Let your servant find favor in your sight.'" (I Samuel 1:18a)

In Divine Hands

She turned to God—
        left burden there—
        felt the assurance
        of answered prayer.

No guarantee—
        just faith ignited;
        her God had heard,
        and fear subsided.

Her hope rekindled,
        and, in the well
        of God's all knowing,
        uncertainty fell.

She trusted God—
        and what that meant
        was faithful acceptance
        of what God sent.

Thought for the Day: How can we say we trust God if we fail to believe that all things work for good after we've placed the matter in divine hands?

NOVEMBER 24

Scripture Reading: Luke 16:10-15

Verse for the Day: "If then you have not been faithful with the dishonest wealth, who will entrust to you the true riches?" (Luke 16:11)

Priorities

Life is a searching for riches,
of treasures. Ah, but what kind?
The things that moths can destroy
or deposits of wealth for the mind?

Draperies, rugs, and clothing,
threatened by varmints and such,
extensions of ego soon worn thin,
or out-dated by style out-of-touch.

There are things that rust can ruin,
just look at the junkyards all filled
with old beat-up cars once driven;
such status their newness instilled.

Then, there are things often stolen;
our vaults cannot keep thieves away.
Our stocks, our bonds, and our monies,
the market re-values each day.

Our values have been so distorted;
the one thing we'll take when we go—
our soul—is often neglected.
Lord knows, it ought not be so!

Thought for the Day: Today I should decide what is really important to me and concentrate on that. Everything else will fall into its proper place if God comes first.

NOVEMBER 25

Scripture Reading: Romans 7:15-25

Verse for the Day: "Wretched man that I am! Who will rescue me from this body of death? Thanks be to God through Jesus Christ our Lord!" (Romans 7:24-25)

Thanksgiving Prayer

For life abundant in the sea;
   for phytoplankton, base of all
the earth's food chain supporting me,
   I thank you, Lord, and humbly call
upon your children everywhere
   to recognize that creatures living
in ocean depths or in the air
   are, in themselves, cause for thanksgiving.
When spotted owl or baby seal
   cannot survive, and ozone layer
thins so ultra rays bombard and peel
   protection from the earth, my prayer
is that you touch each careless hand
   which throws discarded six-pack rings
where fish are choked and wild bird band
   is silenced, strangling, as it sings.
O, God, of those whose true beliefs
   are that you made the earth and all:
the maple trees, the coral reefs,
   the animals, and us, who call
upon your holy name this day—
   this great Thanksgiving Day of days—
please lead us to discern your way
   of conservation as our praise.

Thought for the Day: Thanksgiving Day is appropriate for examination of our thoughtless and uncaring ways, and the realization of duty to God.

NOVEMBER 26

Scripture Reading: II Thessalonians 1:3-12

Verse for the Day: "We must always give thanks to God for you, brothers and sisters, as is right, because your faith is growing abundantly, and the love of everyone of you for one another is increasing." (II Thessalonians 1:3)

Growth Abundant

Which child deserves to be loved?
Which one is worthy of learning?
What little one should have good food?
Which needs a home for returning?

Where should the line of hope be drawn?
When should a soft, cool compress
be offered to soothe a fevered brow?
Who deserves more? Who less?

What youngster has a right to sing—
to wear warm clothes in the winter?
Who is worthy of sitting down
while some must stand if they enter?

Where love of one another stays
the hand of partiality,
there, love of God is evident,
for God's love speaks neutrality.

Thought for the Day: God is not partial; real love does not draw lines or build fences. To be Christ-like is to grow abundantly in love for one another.

NOVEMBER 27

Scripture Reading: Psalm 72:15-19

Verse for the Day: "Blessed be the Lord, the God of Israel, who alone does wondrous things. Blessed be his glorious name forever; may his glory fill the whole earth. Amen and amen." (Psalm 72:18-19)

For the Fall

I come to the mountains in fall—
      when the red leaves on trees
      look like strawberry jam,
      and those blown-down, yellowed
      like brown-sugar yams—
and in wonder I fondly recall

how the season of Thanksgiving comes
      when the colors are rich
      like spun gold in the sky,
      and the weather is perfect
      for fresh pumpkin pie,
and the joy of the harvest just hums

within thankful hearts blessed by all
      that here in the mountains
      mark this special season
      designed by God's hand
      and shaped in God's reason,
and given to earth as the fall.

Thought for the Day: The beauty of the landscape in fall is God's artistry on the canvass of earth. I will take time today to appreciate it.

NOVEMBER 28

Scripture Reading: Amos 7:1-9

Verse for the Day: "Then the Lord said, 'See, I am setting a plumb line in the midst of my people Israel.'" (Amos 7:8a)

With Conscience in Plumb

The Lord's plumb line is justice,
according to old Amos,
and righteousness that flows down
like a stream,
exposing crooked structures
and slicing through those measures
not accurate, not true, not
on the beam.
The Lord's plumb line is lowered
on each of us and ours
who tolerate distortion
of the right—
concerned that there is nothing
divided in our nature,
unjust about our action
or insight.
Behold Christ is the plumb line
revealing faulty building,
correcting costly judgment,
righting wrong.
What does the plumb line tell us
about our own behavior?
Perhaps what conscience told us
all along.

Thought for the Day: Conscience will provide a sure measure of conduct if it's kept in close touch with God, being monitored by the plumb line of Christ.

NOVEMBER 29

Scripture Reading: I Peter 2:1-10

Verse for the Day: "But you are a chosen race, a royal priesthood, a holy nation, God's own people, in order that you may proclaim the mighty acts of him who called you out of darkness into his marvelous light." (I Peter 2:9)

The Promised Role

To some, life's a game of charades
    or a Disneyland parade
or an animated cartoon strip
    with characters all afraid.
Afraid of what they see;
    afraid to stay or flee;
afraid of death at time to come
    or what has yet to be.
But most of all afraid
    of missing the parade,
of slipping out of character
    and forgetting the charade.
But when the thespian soul
    assumes it's promised role—
as child of God, a part of Creation's
    all-encompassing goal ...
then, all else will be right,
    and fear give way to sight.
The choice is ours; we play our part
    in darkness or with light.

Thought for the Day: The life directed by God is the role each of us was meant to fill, however big or little the part. In that role, there is nothing to fear.

NOVEMBER 30

Scripture Reading: Romans 14:19-23

Verse for the Day: "Blessed are those who have no need to condemn themselves because of what they approve." (Romans 14:22b)

Lost and Found

"In time we hate that which we often fear."
The meaning of this line from Shakespeare's pen
is one which vast experience makes clear—
fear eats at one till sanity wears thin.

The hate that fuels religious war and feeds
the constant clash of culture, class, and race
is that same hate which grows from tiny seed
of fear that I'm unworthy of God's grace.

If I feel less than loved, or you feel such,
the wrath we think that we, ourselves, deserve
is centered in a target we can touch—
reduce in stature, punish, or unnerve.

But love for those about us is the end
of knowing God within us as a friend.

Thought for the Day: Those who mistreat or misuse others probably feel in themselves the pain and fear of being lost. To be found is to experience God's love, which casts out fear.

COMES DECEMBER

December

DECEMBER 1

Scripture Reading: Luke 2:1-7

Verse for the Day: "And she gave birth to her firstborn son and wrapped him in bands of cloths, and laid him in a manger, because there was no place for them in the inn." (Luke 2:7)

When Cynicism Takes a Holiday

Though the world becomes very cynical,
we still need to believe in something good:
in holidays hallowed and mystical—
in honesty, hope, peace, and brotherhood.
And just when it seems that we need it most
December arrives under mistletoe;
we're smiling at strangers; serving as host
to parties of friends; old empty lots grow
Christmas tree gardens; the homes on the blocks
have circled porches and windows with light.
Angels with silk wings and shepherds in smocks
balance on floats as they glide through the night.
Christmas is coming and its warm embrace
melts cynicism with unreserved grace.

Thought for the Day: When the world grows too cynical, Christmas arrives, and still, with all its manmade glitter, there is something so basic, simple, and profound that even cynicism takes a holiday.

DECEMBER 2

Scripture Reading: Exodus 3:1-12

Verse for the Day: "There the angel of the Lord appeared in a flaming fire out of a bush; he looked, and the bush was blazing, yet it was not consumed." (Exodus 3:2)

The Encounter

I had a mystical encounter with the Lord
I prayed, "Lord, speak to me while this,
your servant waits for you."
And, suddenly, from deep within I felt
a stirring of my consciousness.
And then, an urge to "do"
came over me—but what to do?
My mind was flooded with
what seemed the Will of God.
I cried, "Lord, I'm the one who is in need!"
The Lord's response ... "Of course you are,
my child, and with my gentle prod,
you'll find your need is met as you
get lost in service to the dispossessed
and those who need a friend."
For just that instant God and I were one!
Now, I'll not question further,
but go wherever the Will may send.

Thought for the Day: From the "burning bush" to the "angel's message," God's guidance comes in many ways. But an encounter with the Almighty is possible and is always life-changing.

DECEMBER 3

Scripture Reading: Matthew 10:26-31

Verse for the Day: "Are not two sparrows sold for a penny? Yet not one of them falls to the ground apart from your Father." (Matthew 10:29)

The Sparrow and Me

Tiny sparrows line the telephone wire;
the cold can't drive them south when they aspire
to be survivors—as all others flee—
role models for mortals like you and me.

I'm often tempted to run and hide,
go south when storm moods throw me off stride.
When winds of rejection blow cold through my bones,
I want to take refuge in temperate zones.

Even geese overhead aligned in a "V,"
while heading south claim victory;
but I must stay and face the chill—
must take my cue from sparrow which will

soon be scavaging on frosty ground
to find what nourishment can be found.
Even so, I know that God will be
close by to comfort the sparrow and me.

Thought for the Day: If even the tiny sparrow is included in God's providential care, I know I am in the sphere of divine concern.

DECEMBER 4

Scripture Reading: Colossians 2:1-7

Verse for the Day: "As you therefore have received Christ Jesus the Lord, continue to live your lives in him ..." (Colossians 2:6)

December Prayer

Dear Lord of December
     (and each month of the year)
this day I'll remember
     and hold very near—
when specter of winter,
     with snow clouds abound
when hardly a splinter
     of sunshine is found—
the rays of your favors
     that shine through the gloom,
that brought without wavers
     new life from the tomb.
As birth of the Christ-child
     reminds us again—
despite rumors run wild
     that commerce will win—
there is a redemption
     for each human heart
where greed finds preemption
     and love gets a start.
So, Lord of December,
     with Christmas upon us
please let yuletide ember
     spark love's year-long bonus.

Thought for the Day: December will be special to my life as lived through out the whole year if I make each day in the month a spiritual step toward Christmas.

DECEMBER 5

Scripture Reading: Romans 11:33-36

Verse for the Day: "O the depth of the riches and wisdom and knowledge of God. How unsearchable are his judgments and how inscrutable his ways." (Romans 11:33)

Thank You, God

Thank you, God, that in winter's gray,
Christmas comes to brighten the way

as colored lights and beaming smiles
bring sunshine to the weary miles

and sparkle to the labored chores
of workers in and out-of-doors

who create dazzling store displays
and guide us through the traffic maze;

who make the meals we all will share;
who wrap the gifts and place them there

beneath the tree whose tinselled bough
and lighted limb our homes endow

with lively hope that when all's done
we'll each be closer to the One

whose love dispels the day's discord—
whom Christmas celebrates as Lord.

Thought for the Day: Each day of December brings closer the moment of truth, when we have to acknowledge what we're celebrating or ignore all together the meaning of Christmas.

DECEMBER 6

Scripture Reading: I John 5:1-5

Verse for the Day: "And this is the victory that conquers the world, our faith." (I John 5:4b)

Just Watch!

Who throws the clouds like pillows through the skies,
sends snowflakes—each a crystal filigree,
puts mischief in a little fellow's eyes,
makes "love" so real the blind can even see?

Who shared with all the world the Christmas song,
placed angels in the heavens overhead,
brought wise men on their journey through the long
star-guided night to hay-strewn manger bed.

Well, I believe the answer's found in hearts
which cannot help but open as the time
of Christmas season celebration starts,
and all of God's creation seems to rhyme.

For those who are inclined to live in doubt,
just watch as Christmas once more comes about!

Thought for the Day: If ever there were a time when the promise that faith will conquer the world seems near to reality, it's at Christmas.

DECEMBER 7

Scripture Reading: Luke 10:57-62

Verse for the Day: "No one who puts a hand to the plow and looks back is fit for the kingdom of heaven." (Luke 10:62)

No Regrets

The land is being cleared,
so nothing on it grows,
but just before the bush was cut
I saved a bright, red rose.

Though it won't live for long,
I saved a rose today,
and I was blessed by loveliness
beyond all pay.

Just think of all the gifts
that we could ever get,
and none beats life lived so that there
is no regret.

Today I saved a rose ...
was all that could be done;
but if I save one rose each day ...
regrets? ... there will be none.

Thought for the Day: Often we think there is so little we can do individually. But we can do the "little" every day, and in so doing accomplish a lot.

DECEMBER 8

Scripture Reading: Matthew 2:13-15

Verse for the Day: "... an angel of the Lord appeared to Joseph in a dream and said, 'Get up, take the child and his mother, and flee to Egypt, and remain there until I tell you for Herod is about to search for the child to destroy him.'" (Matthew 2:13b)

Angels

I have never seen an angel,
but I've no doubt angels exist.
And I believe one will appear
at just the instant life is kissed
by death. An angel plucks the soul
from human form as bullet's aim
is struck. And just between the bridge
abutment and the car, to claim
the unscarred soul, an angel's touch
is felt. Before the water's pitch
consumes last breath, an angel's arms
have lifted soul out of the ditch.
When pain has rendered life as lived
untenable, an angel's song
entices soul to leave the bounds
of failing flesh and sing along.

Though inhumanity exists
and ruthless acts of sabotage,
the innocent can rest assured
no mortal ruse can camouflage
or circumvent Creation's cause,
for still Divinity holds sway
by sending angels to death's door
to lift the soul out of harm's way.

Thought for the Day: An angel's work must surely be to help, and when death is inevitable we can rightly feel that the God of Christmas would send a rescue for the soul.

DECEMBER 9

Scripture Reading: Psalm 19:1-14

Verse for the Day: "Let the words of my mouth and the meditations of my heart be acceptable to you, O Lord, my rock and my redeemer." (Psalm 19:14)

My Spirit Home

I feel I know these woods quite well.
It's here my spirit likes to dwell
when I am trapped in traffic's maze
or when in cloistered office cell.

In **spring** I make a soul's retreat
to hear bird song and feel the sweet,
warm-scented breezes through my hair
and in the stream to soak my feet.

When stifling heat plagues **summer** night,
I come, if only in mind's flight,
to swim the creek where fish abound
and sleep with only stars in sight.

I grow most restless in the **fall**
and need its message most of all.
The red and gold and burnished orange
shout, "Come, be free of roof and wall."

Then, making virgin tracks, I roam
in silent worship under dome
of tree limbs, bare, except for snow,
when **winter** calls my spirit home.

Thought for the Day: God's wonderful creativity and artistry is nowhere if not in the seasons enjoyed by the earth—each a meditation in itself.

DECEMBER 10

Scripture Reading: Proverbs 21:1-8

Verse for the Day: "All deeds are right in the sight of the doer, but the Lord weighs the heart." (Proverbs 21:3)

Weighing the Heart

When King Herod asked the Magi
to tell him where the child
was born, his motive was malice
grown in a heart made wild
by insecurity and fear.
God, having weighed the heart
of Herod—its evil bent shown—
let the Magi depart
another way. Word is, all deeds
are right to the doer,
but the Lord weighs the heart and knows
if motives are pure.

Thought for the Day: Today I will search my own heart for hidden motives, which are never hidden from God, but often from myself and others.

DECEMBER 11

Scripture Reading: Psalm 143:1-12

Verse for the Day: "Teach me to do your will, for you are my God. Let your spirit lead me on a level path." (Psalm 143:10)

The Saint

Prays for God's will;
God's children, a passion;
thanks God for salvation;
thinks prayer is in fashion.

Hands folded in prayer;
knees toughened by kneeling;
strength sapped by demands, but
a warm heart, revealing

faith that the God
of infinite power
will make the path level
if faithful each hour.

Deep trust as a fact;
real love, evident;
a witness, genuine;
an assurance, heaven-sent.

Thought for the Day: Life is a series of ups and downs, a roller-coaster which takes God's spirit to bring about a leveling of the path that leads us to peace of mind.

DECEMBER 12

Scripture Reading: Matthew 1:18-25

Verse for the Day: "... an angel of the Lord appeared to him in a dream and said, 'Joseph, son of David, do not be afraid to take Mary as your wife for the child conceived in her is of the Holy Spirit ...'" (Matthew 1:20b)

When Christmas Is the Norm

When the whole world lives
like each day is Christmas Eve;
when love like Christmas star
lights every sky;
when smiles are as genuine
as children who believe
in Santa and don't question
how or why;
when folks share Christmas hope
because they cannot keep
the joy they feel locked up
in hearts set free;
when souls are so atuned
to angel voice and song
that music fills the earth
with harmony;
when Christmas is the norm,
and daily charity
then this old globe will hang
on heaven's Christmas tree!

Thought for the Day: A spiritual life was obvious in Joseph or he would not have been receptive to the angel's voice. The Christmas spirit ought to be "normal" for us.

DECEMBER 13

Scripture Reading: Matthew 2:16-23

Verse for the Day: "When Herod saw that he had been tricked by the wise men, he was infuriated, and he sent and killed all the children in and around Bethlehem who were two years old or under, according to the time that he had learned from the wise men." (Matthew 2:16)

When It's Over

When December's come and gone
will my memories be such
that I know I've spent too much,
been an all-too-willing pawn
of commercialism's drive?
Have I sold out to the craze
of materialistic maze—
kept idolatry alive?

Or, have I walked in the light—
kept my celebration true
to the best I know to do—
followed Christmas star, still bright?
When December's come and gone,
will the spirit linger on?

Thought for the Day: Christmas is a matter of the heart, or else, like Herod, we lose its significance in the business of staying on top.

DECEMBER 14

Scripture Reading: I Peter 5:1-5

Verse for the Day: "And all of you must clothe yourselves with humility in your dealings with one another, for 'God opposes the proud, but gives grace to the humble.'" (I Peter 5:5b)

Grace to the Humble

May all your gifts beneath the tree
make every wish you wish come true.
May sweet-faced doll sing melody,
and toy soldier march for you.

On Christmas Eve may guests come 'round,
and punch and cookies taste so good.
May church bells ring with joyful sound,
and star-filled sky crown neighborhood.

On Christmas morning may the snow
have blanketed the trees and lawn;
may reindeer tracks appear to show
the wonder of this blessed dawn.

May Christmas celebration leave
the priceless gift you cannot see:
the child-like power to believe—
the spirit of humility.

Thought for the Day: Let me realize anew this day that Christmas is not just for children. It is God's way of re-entering the heart.

DECEMBER 15

Scripture Reading: Matthew 28:16-20

Verse for the Day: "And remember, I am with you always, to the end of the age." (Matthew 28:20b)

God's Sacred Vow

Christmas is a gift transcending
all human understanding!
Beyond our puny comprehending
is this blessed day, demanding
God's most gracious condescension,
meeting mortals as we play
at living life in full dimension,
yet, often choosing to stray
as far from pious as the mind
will take us; using the Lord
when troubles and foolishness find
us turning plowshear into sword,
then ignoring the Almighty
when good fortune has a run.
But Christmas comes to let us see
once more God incarnate as Son—
that we, though plagued by wayward trend,
might hear, in Christ, God's sacred vow
to be with us—a stalwart friend—
in all life's moments ... even now.

Thought for the Day: To stray from the moral highground is the easy thing to do. To be true to the message of Christmas demands daily adjustment to God's presence.

DECEMBER 16

Scripture Reading: Revelation 7:9-17

Verse for the Day: "... for the Lamb at the center of the throne will be their shepherd, and he will guide them to springs of the water of life, and God will wipe away every tear from their eyes." (Revelation 7:17)

Celebration To Come

The Christmas celebration,
if you're standing on the side,
can create some real anxiety
which cannot be denied.

For the glitter of the tinsel
and the sparkle of the lights
can reveal a sorrow hidden
in the long December nights.

To the heart alone and lonely
where despair has taken toll,
all the sentimental music
sounds like thunder in the soul.

But Christ came to bring the message
that resounds as Christmas nears ...
in celestial celebration
God will wipe away all tears.

Thought for the Day: The undeniable fact is that the Christmas celebration can produce feelings of anxiety and sadness for some, but its promise is for all.

DECEMBER 17

Scripture Reading: Luke 2:13-16

Verse for the Day: "Glory to God in the highest heaven, and on earth peace among those whom he favors!" (Luke 2:14)

She Knows

When she first sees the tree
with ornaments and lights
and colored tinseled strings.
and underneath, delights
all wrapped and tied with bows,
her little eyes grow wide,
and mirrored in her smile
is joy from deep inside.

Angelic face haloed
by brown-gold curls and bangs,
her little hands stretch out
for anything that hangs
within her reach. She knows,
somehow instinctively,
that Christmas is for her
and will forever be.

Thought for the Day: Christmas is not just for children, but they're a big part of it. There is something of the baby Jesus in every little child.

DECEMBER 18

Scripture Reading: Jonah 2:1-10

Verse for the Day: "Deliverance belongs to the Lord!" (Jonah 2:9b)

When Grandpa Reads

When winter strikes outside like raging bull,
and snow comes down in sheets of feathered flakes;
when every room inside the house is full,
and all of us are nursing stomach aches
from eating too much rich and spicy food,
then Grandpa gets the Good Book and suggests
that all of his world-wise, much-traveled brood
should take time at this annual family-fest
to listen to the story from St. Luke
of why it is each year the whole world waits
for Christmas—coming as divine rebuke
of evil with its store of fear and hate.
I hear the voice of God from heaven's rim
when Grandpa reads of Christ in Bethlehem.

Thought for the Day: The Christmas story is the continuation of God's deliverance and listening to it as a family is one of the most important traditions we can help to establish.

DECEMBER 19

Scripture Reading: Micah 4:1-5

Verse for the Day: "For out of Zion shall go forth instruction, and the word of the Lord from Jerusalem." (Micah 4:2b)

The Word

We've unpacked all decorations,
    unwrapped the ornaments,
created one gigantic mess
    of gaudy ambience.

We've shopped for toys and clothes and junk,
    spent all our hard-earned cash;
from party to party it has been
    one frantic, head-long dash.

We're totally undone before
    the after-Christmas "down."
Why is it we let artifice
    wear the December crown?

The birth of Christ was simple fare—
    a manger in a stall.
The Word that came from Bethlehem
    was "least" is best of all.

Thought for the Day: We need to stay close to the Scriptural depiction of Christmas if the celebration is to be the life revitalization it's meant to be.

DECEMBER 20

Scripture Reading: Micah 5:1-5

Verse for the Day: "But you, O Bethlehem of Ephrathah, who are one of the little clans of Judah, from you shall come forth for me one who is to rule Israel ... and he shall be the one of peace." (Micah 5:la, 5b)

The One

Christmas—really Christmas—
is not the glitter and glare
of colored lights and tinseled trees,
but open hearts that share.

Christmas—merry Christmas—
is not on toy store shelves,
but in the twinkle of the eyes
of those who give themselves.

Christmas—happy Christmas—
in not in Santa Claus,
as jolly as he makes us feel,
he's only here because

of Christmas—blessed Christmas—
that is not wrapped as a token,
but as a tiny new-born
through whom the Lord has spoken.

Thought for the Day: When the celebration is over and the merriment is packed away, what we will remember is the impact of Christmas on our hearts. Let that be one of blessing.

DECEMBER 21

Scripture Reading: Micah 6:1-8

Verse for the Day: "... and what does the Lord require of you but to do justice, and to love kindness, and to walk humbly with your God." (Micah 6:8b)

The Question

Could God have fashioned in one child
salvation for a world defiled?
Could Mary there have known her son
was born to be the promised One?
Could Joseph ever understand
the portent of a scheme so grand?
Could shepherds in their humble guise
rely on message from the skies?
Could wise men from a distance far
trust guidance from a strange, new star?
Could Christ have known, or could he see
beyond that star to thorn-crowned tree?
Could I explain how I have failed
to practice justice; often railed
unkindly and in pride ignored
the humble walk with Christ, my Lord?

Thought for the Day: Considering the import of the Christmas experience, practicing justice, loving kindness, and walking humbly with God does not seem too much to ask.

DECEMBER 22

Scripture Reading: Micah 7:1-9

Verse for the Day: "... when I sit in darkness, the Lord will be a light to me... He will bring me out to the light; I shall see his vindication." (Micah 7:8b, 9b)

The Light

The Light that shines from the manger
is strong enough to lighten
the path to peace for all who use
its brilliant beam to brighten
each day and live in hallowed stream
of radiance from the Child.
The Light is strong enough to drive
from mind the shadowed, wild,
night fears made real by lack of sight.
Its glow is broad enough
to push trespassing dread away,
call lurking anger's bluff.
The peace illumined by the One
in manger sweetly napping
is God's own Christmas gift which all
Creation's still unwrapping.

Thought for the Day: The symbol of light at Christmas, in and around our homes, is inspired by Christ, the Light of the world. Christmas is God's calling us to the Light!

DECEMBER 23

Scripture Reading: Luke 2:17-33

Verse for the Day: "But Mary treasured all these words and pondered them in her heart." (Luke 2:19)

Christmas to Keep

It was the day before
the day before Christmas—
Christmas Eve eve to be exact.
All preparations for
the Day were completed ...
all plans for surprise were in tact.
The air waves were filled with
the world's favorite carols;
the music was all joyful sound.
The presents were gift-wrapped;
name tags were inserted.
There wasn't a Scrooge to be found.
The twenty-third morning
of lovely December
broke bright—not a cloud in the sky.
There suddenly came to
my mind—I was guilty
of passing the Christ child right by.
So I spent the day at
the Children's Hospital
rocking some angels to sleep.
And now I know Christmas
will be even better,
for it's in my heart to keep.

Thought for the Day: The real spirit of Christmas is that which is treasured in the heart and touches others. Do I have the Christmas spirit yet? Will it keep?

DECEMBER 24

Scripture Reading: Luke 3:1-6

Verse for the Day: "He went into all the region around Jordan, proclaiming a baptism of repentance for the forgiveness of sins, as it is written in the book of the words of the prophet Isaiah, 'The voice of one crying in the wilderness: Prepare the way of the Lord, make his paths straight.'" (Luke 3:3,4)

The Most Unlikely

Sometimes the biggest news comes from
the most unlikely source.
"Repent, God is at hand!" John called
from wilderness. Of course,
his message was to set the scene
for Christ, the One whom he
would recognize as sent from God in
response to prophesy.

Remember that the Lord, himself—
the good news at its best—
had come in humble setting as
a new-born laid to rest
in a stable where the cattle
ate and lambs would play.
Sometimes the biggest news comes in
the most unlikely way.

Thought for the Day: To those who humbly receive ... humility opens the door to the child-like within us that lets us receive the good news, however it comes.

DECEMBER 25

Scripture Reading: John 14:1-7

Verse for the Day: "Jesus said to him, 'I am the way, and the truth, and the life.'" (John 14:6a)

God Gave the World

What is there about Christmas that makes it
unlike any other day of the year?
If Christmas is "happy," it's happier—
filled with more warm-hearted good will and cheer
than the other three-hundred sixty-four.
But, if it's "sad," it's sadder than the rest—
and lonelier and more heart-breaking, for
Christmas time has come to be the test
of family fidelity and love.
But families were meant to change; it's so
we'll not rely on earthly ties to bind
our hearts in hope, but will, instead, let go.
       And then get hold of Christmas as the day
       God gave the world the life, the truth, the way.

Thought for the Day: The real spirit of Christmas is not found beneath the Christmas tree where hands grab for gifts, but at the manger where hearts are grabbed by the gift.

DECEMBER 26

Scripture Reading: Matthew 2:7-12

Verse for the Day: "... having been warned in a dream not to return to Herod, they left for their own country by another road." (Matthew 2:12)

Another Way

The wise men knew
of Herod's plot—
by God alerted.
They journeyed home
by other roads—
king's plan averted.

With gold and myrrh
and frankincense
laid at the manger,
they knelt to pray
in tribute to
the tiny stranger.

Then God who led
them to this truth
took them home again
But, they went back
another way.
Forever—changed men!

Thought for the Day: An encounter with Christ will send us back to the world another way ... changed in attitude and outlook.

DECEMBER 27

Scripture Reading: Mark 7:1-8

Verse for the Day: "You abandon the commandment of God and hold to human tradition." (Mark 7:8)

A New Tradition

I always send a Christmas card
to each name on my list
and nearly faint if I get one
from somebody I've missed.

I can't remember half the people—
the list has grown so long,
but if I didn't send each one,
I'd feel, somehow, all wrong.

I know I ought to write a note—
but I find that a chore;
besides I think my odd tidbits
of personal news a bore.

A new "tradition" might be best—
to send, throughout the year,
a card each day to those whose names
on no one's list appear.

Thought for the Day: Sometimes traditions can become stressful and unworthy, their original purpose lost in the ordeal. Something innovative might be more in the spirit.

DECEMBER 28

Scripture Reading: Matthew 2:1-6

Verse for the Day: "Where is the child who has been born king of the Jews? For we observed his star at its rising and have come to pay him homage." (Matthew 2:2)

Where Is the Child?

We saw his star—
that beam of heavenly light
which brought the Magi
through the long, dark night.

We heard the angels sing—
the heavenly band that spilled
across the midnight sky,
as shepherd path was filled
with songs of peace on earth.

But where's the child?
We did not see the manger—
the cattle nearby, mild-
mannered and patient—
the mother's warm smile
inviting all to see,
to linger yet awhile.
Where is the child?

His grimy, tear-streaked, sweet
innocence is cradled in a box
near the busy city street.

Thought for the Day: The enchantment of the first Christmas scene often blinds us to the all-too-real facts surrounding us. Christ comes into a hostile world.

DECEMBER 29

Scripture Reading: Luke 4:16-21

Verse for the Day: "The Spirit of the Lord is upon me, because he has sent me to bring good news to the poor. He has sent me to proclaim release to the captives and recovery of sight to the blind, to let the oppressed go free, to proclaim the year of the Lord's favor." (Luke 4:18-19)

The Jubilee Year

> Until Christ came just once each fifty
>   years was Jubilee.
> And then all debts were cancelled, and all
>   prisoners set free.
> Resentments were forgiven, and old
>   grudges were set by;
> long-held disputes and family feuds
>   were allowed to die.
>
> Land-holdings were restored to those who
>   rightfully held claim.
> Each fallen in disgrace was given
>   back his own good name.
> Forgiveness was a fact of life just
>   once each fifty years;
> but every year is Jubilee when
>   Jesus Christ appears.
>
> Each year—its every day—for those
>   forgiven and set free
> becomes the "favored" of the Lord—
>   the Year of Jubilee!

Thought for the Day: Forgiveness is the one gift offered by God which we must give away if we are to receive. I will live the new year as a forgiving and forgiven person.

DECEMBER 30

Scripture Reading: Psalm 42:1-11

Verse for the Day: "As a deer longs for flowing streams, so my soul longs for you, O God." (Psalm 42:1)

A Spot Within

There is a need, as year is closed,
that new year can fulfill—
a longing to draw nearer to
the One who can instill
within the soul a peace sublime,
tranquility divine—
a need to keep a spot within
where ego can enshrine
its Creator until all else
is seen through eyes that glow
with reverent, devoted love
through what may come and go.

Throughout the coming year let new
resolve unite the days
that there's reserved within my heart
a spot for constant praise.

Thought for the Day: The closer one stays to a state of praise, the more realization there is of what can be accomplished by a life of devotion.

DECEMBER 31

Scripture Reading: Luke 11:25-30

Verse for the Day: "For my yoke is easy, and my burden is light." (Luke 11:30)

Starting Over

The ending of the year,
like the closing of a book
when the final chapter's read,
leaves little to be said,
except one final look
back at what is now quite clear.

Then, it's on to something new—
something better than before.
Leave what's over in its place
as experience of grace;
open wide the future's door,
see the sky as bright and blue.

Ready with compassion's touch;
keeping God in mind each day;
living so there's no regret;
willing to forgive, forget;
sharing with the world a ray
of the light it needs so much.

Thought for the Day: The threshold of a new year is the ideal time to discover that Christianity is easier on the human spirit than other lifestyles because of God's promised support.

Printed in the United States
36556LVS00004B/37-78

9 781591 291442